The Mystery of the Strange Messages

Enid Blyton

The Mystery of the Strange Messages

ARMADA

First published in the UK in 1961
by Methuen & Co. Ltd
Republished by Dragon Books in 1969
First published in Armada in 1988
This impression 1989

Armada is an imprint of
the Children's Division, part of
the Collins Publishing Group,
8 Grafton Street, London W1X 3LA

Printed and bound in Great Britain by
William Collins Sons & Co. Ltd, Glasgow

Mr. Goon is Angry

Mr. Goon, the village policeman, was in a very bad temper. He sat at his desk, and stared at three pieces of paper there, spread out before him. Beside them were three cheap envelopes.

On each sheet of paper separate words were pasted in uneven lines. "They're all words cut out of some newspaper," said Mr. Goon. "So's the writer's handwriting wouldn't give him away, I suppose! And what nonsense they make – look at this one now – 'TURN HIM OUT OF THE IVIES!' What does *that* mean, I'd like to know. And this one – 'ASK SMITH WHAT HIS REAL NAME IS.' Who's Smith?"

He stared at the last piece of paper. "CALL YOURSELF A POLICEMAN? BETTER GO AND SEE SMITH."

"Gah!" said Mr. Goon. "Better put them all into the waste-paper basket!" He took one of the envelopes and looked at it. It was a very cheap one, square in shape, and on each one was pasted two words only.

Mr. goon.

Each word was pasted separately, as if cut from a newspaper. Goon's surname had no capital letter, and he nodded his head at that.

"Must be a fellow with no education that put my name with a small letter," he said. "What's he mean – all this business about some place called The Ivies, and a fellow called Smith? Must be mad! Rude too – 'Call myself a policeman!' I'll tell him a few things when I see him."

He gave a sudden shout. "Mrs. Hicks! Come here a minute, will you?"

Mrs. Hicks, the woman who came in to clean for Mr. Goon, shouted back, "Let me wipe me hands and I'll be there!"

Mr. Goon frowned. Mrs. Hicks treated him as if he were an ordinary man, not a policeman, whose frown ought to send her scuttling, and whose voice ought to bring her in at top speed. After a minute or two she arrived, panting as if she had run for miles.

"Just in the middle of washing-up," she began. "And I think I'd better tell you, Mr. Goon, you want a couple of new cups, and a . . ."

"I've no time to talk about crockery," said Mr. Goon, snappily. "Now see here . . ."

"And me tea-cloth is just about in rags," went on Mrs. Hicks. "How I'm supposed to wash up with . . ."

"MRS. HICKS! I called you in on an official matter," said the policeman, sternly.

"All right, all right," said Mrs. Hicks, in a huff. "What's up? If you want my advice on that fellow who goes round stealing the vegetables off our allotments, well, I can give a good guess. I . . ."

"Be quiet, woman," said Mr. Goon, fiercely, wishing he could clap her into a cell for an hour or two. "I merely want to ask you a few questions."

"What about? I've done nothing wrong," said Mrs. Hicks, a little alarmed at Goon's angry face.

"Look – see these three letters you brought in to me?" said Goon, pushing the envelopes over towards Mrs. Hicks. "Well, where exactly did you find them? You said one was in the coal-shed, on the shovel."

"That's right," said Mrs. Hicks, "set right in the middle of the shovel it was. And all it said on the envelope was 'Mr goon' and I brought it straight into you today."

"And where did you say the others were?" asked Mr. Goon, in his most official manner.

"Well, one come in through the letter-box some time," said Mrs. Hicks, "and you weren't in so I put it on your desk. And the second one was on the dustbin lid, sir –

6

stuck there with a bit of sticky paper. Couldn't help but see it when I went to empty the dustpan. And what I say is, it's pretty queer to have notes all . . ."

"Yes, yes," said Mr. Goon. "Have you seen anyone sneaking about round the back? Somebody must have climbed over the fence to put the notes in the coal-shed and on the dustbin."

"I haven't seen no one," said Mrs. Hicks, "and what's more if I had, I'd have taken my broom and given him a whack on the head. What's in the notes, sir – anything important?"

"No," said Mr. Goon. "It's probably all just a silly joke – you don't know of any place here called The Ivies, do you?"

"The Ivies?" said Mrs. Hicks, considering. "No, I don't. Sure you don't mean 'The Poplars,' sir? Now, a nice gentleman lives there, sir, I do for him each Friday when I don't come to you, and he's ever so nice to me, he . . ."

"I said the *Ivies*, not the Poplars," said Mr. Goon. "All right. You can go, Mrs. Hicks. But keep an eye on the back garden, will you? I'd like to get a description of whoever it is leaving these notes about the place."

"I will that, sir," said Mrs. Hicks. "And what about me getting you a couple more cups, sir – one broke in my hand, and . . ."

"Oh, *get* the cups," said Mr. Goon. "And I don't want to be disturbed for the next hour. I've important work to do!"

"So've I," said Mrs. Hicks. "That kitchen stove of yours is just crying out for a good clean and . . ."

"Well, go and stop it crying," snapped Mr. Goon, and heaved a sigh of relief as Mrs. Hicks disappeared in a huff.

He studied the three notes again, puzzling over the cut-out, pasted on words. What newspaper had they been cut from? It would be a help to find out, but Goon could see no way of discovering that. Who had sent them – and why? There wasn't any place called "The Ivies" in Peterswood.

He took up a local directory of roads and houses again, and went through it carefully. Then he picked up the telephone receiver.

When the exchange answered he asked for the postmaster. "P.C. Goon here," he said, importantly, and at once he was put through to the right department.

"Er – Postmaster," said Goon, "I want a little information, please. Is there a house – possibly a new one – called The Ivies here in Peterswood?"

"The Ivies?" said the Postmaster. "Let me think – Ivies. No, there isn't, Mr. Goon. There's The Poplars, though, that might be . . ."

"It is *not* The Poplars," said Goon. "I'm also looking for someone called Smith, who . . ."

"Smith? Oh, I can give you the addresses of at least fifteen Smiths in Peterswood," said the Postmaster. "Do you want them now?"

"No, I don't," said Mr. Goon, desperately, and put down the receiver with a bang. He gazed at the three notes again. No address on them. No name at the bottom. Where did they come from? Who had sent them? Did they mean anything – or was it a fat-headed joke?

A joke? Who would dare to play a joke like that on *him*, P.C. Goon, representative of the law for Peterswood? An uneasy feeling crept over Mr. Goon, as a vision of a plump boy with a broad grin on his face came into his mind.

"That fat boy! Frederick Trotteville!" he said, out loud. "He's home for the holidays – and he won't have gone back to school yet. Gah! That toad of a boy! He'd think it was clever to send me notes like this – sending me off on a false trail – putting me on a wrong scent – deceiving me and making me look for houses called The Ivies. GAH!"

He sat down to do some work, but at the back of his

8

mind was the continual thought that it might be Fatty Trotteville playing a joke, and he found himself unusually slow with the making out of his reports. In the middle of his second report Mrs. Hicks came running in, breathless as usual.

"Mr. Goon, sir – here's another of them notes!" she said, panting as if she had run a mile, and putting another of the familiar square envelopes down on Mr. Goon's desk. He stared at it. Yes – his name was there as usual, pasted on the envelope. "Mr. goon". No capital letter for his surname – so it was obviously from the same sender.

"Did you see anyone? Where did you find it?" demanded Mr. Goon, slitting it open very carefully.

"Well, I went to hang out my dish-cloth – and a real rag it is too," said Mrs. Hicks. "And when I put my hand into the peg-bag, there was this letter – on top of the pegs!"

"Was anyone about?" asked Mr. Goon.

"No – the only person who's been this morning is the butcher-boy with your chops, sir," said Mrs. Hicks.

"BUTCHER-boy!" said Goon, starting up, and making Mrs. Hicks step backwards in fright. "HO! Now we know where we are! Butcher-boy! Did you see this boy?"

"No, sir. I was upstairs making your bed," said Mrs. Hicks, alarmed at Goon's purple face. "I just called out to him to leave the meat on the table, and he did, because I found it there, and he went off whistling, and . . ."

"All right. That's enough. I know all I want to know now," said Goon. "I'm going out, Mrs. Hicks, so answer the telephone for me till I'm back. And you'll be glad to know that's the last of these notes you'll find. Butcher-boy! I'll butcher-boy him! I'll . . ."

"But Charlie Jones is a *good* lad!" said Mrs. Hicks. "He's the best boy the butcher ever had, he told me so. He . . ."

"I'm not thinking of Charlie Jones," said Mr. Goon, putting on his helmet, and adjusting the strap. "Ho no –

9

I'm thinking of someone else! And that someone else is going to get a Nasty Shock."

Mrs. Hicks was puzzled and curious, but not another word would Mr. Goon say. He strode out of his office, fetched his bicycle and rode off. In his pocket were the four notes he had received. He thought over the fourth one as he rode down the street. Ten words, cut out from newspapers again, and pasted on the sheet. "You'll be sorry if you don't go and see Smith."

"It's that fat boy, Frederick Trotteville, I'm certain it is," thought Goon, pedalling fast. "Ha – he disguised himself as a butcher-boy again, did he? Well, he's done that before, and he's made a great mistake doing it again! I can see through you, you toad of a boy! Wasting my time with idiotic notes! I've got you this time. You just wait!"

He turned in at Fatty's gate, and rode up the drive to the house. At once a small Scottie raced out of the bushes, barking gleefully at the policeman's ankles.

"You clear orf!" shouted Mr. Goon, and kicked out at the delighted dog. "Bad as your master you are! Clear orf, I say!"

"Hallo, Mr. Goon!" said Fatty's voice. "Come here, Buster. You can't treat your best friend like that! You seem in a hurry, Mr. Goon."

The policeman dismounted, his face red with pedalling so furiously. "You keep that dog off me," he said. "I want a word with you, Master Frederick Trotteville. In fact, I want a Long Talk. Ha – you thought you were very clever, didn't you, sending all those notes?"

"I really don't know what you're talking about," said Fatty, puzzled. "But do come in. We'll have a nice cosy chat together!"

10

A New Mystery, Perhaps?

Fatty took Mr. Goon in at the side door and then into the sitting-room. "Is your mother in – or your father?" asked Goon, thinking that it would be good for them to see their wonderful son properly ticked off by him.

"No, they're out," said Fatty. "But Larry and the others are here. I'm sure they would be interested to hear your little tale, whatever it is. We've been a bit dull these holidays, so far – no mystery to solve, Mr. Goon. I suppose you haven't one that you want any help with?"

"You'd talk the hind leg off a donkey, you would," said Mr. Goon, glad to get a word in. "So those friends of yours are here, are they? Yes, you bring them in. Do them good to hear what I've got to say!"

Fatty went to the door and gave such a loud shout that Mr. Goon almost jumped out of his skin. It made Buster come out from under a chair and bark madly. Mr. Goon glared at him.

"You keep away from me, you pest of a dog," he said. "Master Frederick, can't you send that animal out of the room? If he comes near me I'll give him such a kick."

"No, you won't," said Fatty. "You wouldn't want me to report you to the police for cruelty to an animal, would you, Mr. Goon? Buster, sit!"

There was the sound of feet coming down the stairs, and Larry, Daisy, Pip and Bets rushed in, eager to know why Fatty had yelled so loudly. They stopped short when they saw the stout policeman.

"Oh – hallo, Mr. Goon," said Larry, surprised. "What a pleasant surprise!"

"So you're all here, are you?" said Mr. Goon, glaring round. "Hatching mischief as usual, I suppose?"

"Well, not exactly," said Pip. "Fatty's mother is having a jumble sale, and we're turning out the attic for her to see what we can find. Have *you* got any jumble to spare, Mr. Goon – a couple of old helmets that don't fit you, perhaps – they'd sell like hot cakes."

Bets gave a sudden giggle, and then retreated hurriedly behind Fatty as Goon looked sternly at her.

"Sit down, all of you," commanded Mr. Goon. "I've come here about a serious matter. I thought I'd see what you've got to say about it before I report it to Headquarters."

"This sounds very very interesting," said Fatty, sitting on the couch. "Do sit down too, Mr. Goon. Let's all be comfortable and listen to your bedtime story."

"It won't do you any good to be cheeky, Master Frederick, I can tell you that," said Mr. Goon, seating himself majestically in the biggest arm-chair in the room. "No, that it won't. First of all – why weren't you upstairs in the attics with the others?"

Fatty looked astonished. "I brought some jumble downstairs to stack in the garage," he said. "Then I heard old Buster barking and came to see who the visitor was. Why?"

"Ho! Well, let me tell you that *I* know what you've been doing this morning!" said Goon. "You've been putting on that butcher-boy disguise of yours, haven't you? Oh yes, I know all about it! You got out your striped butcher-boy apron, didn't you – and you put on that red wig – and . . ."

"I'm sorry to say that I didn't," said Fatty. "I agree that it would have been much more exciting to parade round as a butcher-boy, than to stagger downstairs with smelly old jumble – but I must be truthful, Mr. Goon. You wouldn't like me to tell a lie, just to please you, would you? I'm afraid I *haven't* been a butcher-boy this morning!"

"Ho! You haven't – so you *say!*" said Mr. Goon, raising his voice. "And I suppose you didn't leave a note in my peg-bag when you came to my house? And you didn't leave one on my coal-shovel and . . ."

Fatty was too astonished for words. So were the others. They looked at one another, wondering uneasily if Mr. Goon had gone mad. Peg-bags? Coal-shovels? What next?

"And I suppose you thought it was *very* clever to stick a note on my dustbin lid?" went on Mr. Goon, his voice growing louder still. He stared round at the silent children, who were all gazing at him, astounded.

"Where will you put the notes next?" he said sarcastically. "Go on, tell me. Where? I'd like to know, then I could look there."

"Well, let's see," said Fatty, frowning hard. "What about inside a watering-can – if you've got one, have you Mr. Goon. Or in your shopping-basket . . ."

"Or on his dressing-table," said Larry, joining in. "He wouldn't have to go and look for a note there. It would be right under his nose."

Mr. Goon had gone purple. He looked round threateningly, and Bets half-thought she would make a dash out of the door. She didn't like Mr. Goon when he looked like that!

"That's not funny," said Mr. Goon, angrily. "Not at all funny. It only makes me more certain than ever that you've planned those silly notes together."

"Mr. Goon, we haven't the least idea what you're talking about," said Fatty, seeing that the policeman really had some serious complaint to do with notes sent to him. "Suppose you tell us what you've come about – and we'll tell you quite honestly whether we know anything about it or not."

"Well, I *know* you're mixed up in it, Master Fredderick," said Goon. "It – it *smells* of you. Just the sort of thing you'd do, to make a bit of fun for the others. But sending anonymous notes isn't funny. It's wrong."

"What are *anonymous* notes?" asked Bets. "I don't quite know."

13

"They're letters sent by someone who is afraid to put his name at the end," explained Fatty. "Usually anonymous notes have no address and no signature – and they're only sent by mean, cowardly people. Isn't that so, Mr. Goon?"

"That is so," said the policeman. "And I tell you straight, Master Frederick, that you've described yourself good and proper, if you sent those notes!"

"Well, I didn't," said Fatty, beginning to lose patience. "For goodness' sake, Mr. Goon, come to the point, and tell us what's happened. We're completely in the dark."

"Oh no, you're not," said Goon, and took the four notes from his pocket, each in their envelopes. He handed them to Fatty, who slid the notes out of their envelopes, one by one, and read them out loud.

"Here's the first note. All it says is 'Ask Smith what his real name is.' And here's the second. 'Turn him out of the Ivies.' And this one says 'Call yourself a policeman? Go and see Smith!' And the last one says 'You'll be sorry if you don't go and see Smith!' Well – what queer notes! Look, all of you – they're not even handwritten!"

He passed them round. "Whoever wrote them cut the words out of newspapers – and then pasted them on the sheets of writing-paper," said Larry. "That's a common trick with people who don't want their writing recognized."

"This is really rather peculiar," said Fatty, most interested. "Who's Smith? And where is the house called 'The Ivies'?"

"Don't know one," said Daisy. "But there's 'The Poplars' – it's in our road."

"Gah!" said Mr. Goon, aggravated to hear "The Poplars" suggested once more. Nobody took any notice of him.

"And there's 'The Firs'," said Bets, "and 'The Chestnuts'. But I can't think of any house called 'The Ivies'."

"And this Mr. Smith," said Fatty, staring at one of the notes. "Why should he have to be turned out of the

14

Ivies, wherever it is? And why should Mr. Goon ask him what his *real* name is? It must be someone going under a false name for some purpose. Most peculiar."

"It *really* sounds like a mystery!" said Pip, hopefully. "We haven't had one this hols. This is exciting."

"And the notes were put into a peg-bag – and on a coal-shovel – and stuck to the dustbin," said Fatty, frowning. "Isn't that what you said, Mr. Goon? Where was the fourth one?"

"*You* know that as well as I do," growled the policeman. "It came through the letter-box. My daily woman, Mrs. Hicks, found them all. And when she told me that the butcher-boy arrived this morning at the same time as the last note – well, I guessed who was at the bottom of all this."

"Well, as *I* wasn't that butcher-boy, why don't you go and question the *real* butcher-boy," said Fatty. "Or shall I? This is jolly interesting, Mr. Goon. I think there's something behind all this!"

"So do I. *You* are, Master Frederick Trotteville!" said Mr. Goon. "Now don't you keep telling me it wasn't you. I know you well enough by now. You'll come to a bad end, you will – telling me fibs like this!"

"I think we'll bring this meeting to an end," said Fatty, "I never tell lies, Mr. Goon, never. You ought to know that by now. I've had my jokes, yes – and played a good many tricks. But I – do – NOT – tell lies! Here – take the letters, and get your bicycle."

Mr. Goon rose up majestically from his arm-chair. He took the letters from Fatty and then threw them violently on the floor.

"You can have them back!" he said, "You sent them, and you can keep them. But mind you – if ONE MORE of those notes arrives at my police-station, I go straight to Superintendent Jenks and report the whole lot."

"I really do think you'd better do that anyhow," said Fatty. "There may be something *serious* behind all this, you know. You've got a bee in your bonnet about me –

I don't know a thing about these anonymous letters. Now please go."

"Why didn't you have the envelopes and the writing-paper inside tested for finger-prints, Mr. Goon?" said Pip, suddenly. "Then you'd have known if Fatty's were there, or not. You could have taken his too, to prove it."

"As it is, we've all handled the notes, and must have messed up any finger-prints that were there already," said Fatty. "Blow!"

"Finger-prints! Bah!" said Goon. "You'd be clever enough to wear *gloves* if you sent anonymous notes, Master Frederick Trotteville. Well, I've said my say, and I'm going. But just you mind my words – ONE MORE NOTE, and you'll get into such trouble that you'll wish you'd never been born. And I should burn that butcher-boy rig-out of yours, if I were you – if it hadn't been for you acting the butcher-boy this morning I'd never have guessed it was you leaving those notes."

He went out of the room and banged the door so violently that Buster barked in astonishment, and ran to the door, scratching at it eagerly.

"Be quiet, Buster," said Fatty, sitting down on the couch again. "I say, you others – what do you think about these notes? A bit queer, aren't they?"

Larry had picked them all up and put them on the table. The five looked at them.

"Do we do a little detective work?" said Larry, eagerly. "Goon's given it up, obviously – shall we take it on?"

"Rather!" said Fatty. "Our next mystery is now be-ginning!"

Mr. Goon is worried

Mr. Goon cycled home, very angry indeed. Fatty always seemed to get the best of him somehow – and yet the policeman felt that he, Goon, had been in the right all the time. That fat boy had given himself away properly by disguising himself as the butcher-boy again. He'd done it once too often this time! Ah well, he could tell Mrs. Hicks that he had solved the business of those notes, and given someone a good ticking-off!

He flung his bicycle against the fence, and went into his house. He found Mrs. Hicks scrubbing the kitchen floor, a soapy mess all round her.

"Oh, there you are, sir," she began, "Look, I'll have to have a new scrubbing-brush, this here one's got no bristles left, and I can't . . ."

"Mrs. Hicks – about those notes," interrupted Mr. Goon. "There won't be any more, you'll be glad to know. I've been to talk to the one who wrote them – frightened him almost to death, I did – he admitted everything, but I've taken a kindly view of the whole matter, and let him off, this time. So there won't be any more."

"Oh, but you're wrong, sir," said Mrs. Hicks, rising up from her knees with difficulty, and standing before him with the dripping scrubbing-brush still in her hand. "You're quite wrong. I found another note, sir, as soon as you'd gone!"

"You couldn't have," said Mr. Goon, taken aback.

"Oh, but I did, sir," said Mrs. Hicks. "And a funny place it was in too. I wouldn't have noticed it if the milkman hadn't pointed it out."

"The milkman? Why, did *he* find it?" said Mr. Goon, astonished. "Where was it?"

17

"Well, sir, it was tucked into the empty milk-bottle, stood outside the back-door," said Mrs. Hicks, enjoying the policeman's surprise. "The milkman picked up the bottle and of course he saw the note at once – it was sticking out of the bottle-neck, sir."

Mr. Goon sat down heavily on a kitchen chair. "When was the note put there?" he asked. "Could it have been slipped in some time ago – say when the butcher-boy was here?"

"Oh no, sir. Why, I'd only put out the milk-bottle a few minutes before the milkman came," said Mrs. Hicks. "I washed it out, sir. I always do wash my milk-bottles out, I don't hand them dirty to the milkman, like *some* folks – and I put it out nice and clean. And about three minutes later along came Joe – that's the milkman, sir – and puts down your quart, sir, and picks up the empty bottle."

"And was the note in it then?" asked Mr. Goon, hardly able to believe it.

"Yes, sir. And the milkman, he says to me, 'Hey, what's this note for? It's addressed to Mr. Goon!' and he gave it to me, sir, and it's on your desk this very minute."

"Exactly when did the milkman hand you the note?" asked poor Mr. Goon.

"About twenty minutes ago, sir," said Mrs. Hicks. Goon groaned. Twenty minutes ago he had been with all five children – so it was plain that not one of them could have been stuffing a note into his empty milk-bottle then. Certainly not Fatty.

"You look upset, sir," said Mrs. Hicks. "Shall I make you a nice hot cup of tea. The kettle's boiling."

"Yes. Yes, I think I could do with one," said Goon, and walked off heavily to his little office. He sat down in his chair.

Now what was he to do? It couldn't have been Fatty after all. There was someone else snooping about, hiding notes here and there when no one was around. And good

18

gracious – he had left all the notes with those five kids! What a thing to do! Mr. Goon brooded for a few minutes and was glad to see Mrs. Hicks coming in with an enormous cup of hot tea.

"I put in four lumps," said Mrs. Hicks. "And there's another in the saucer. You've got a sweet tooth, haven't you, sir? What about me getting a new scrubbing-brush, now we're on the subject, and . . ."

"We're *not* on the subject," said Mr. Goon, shortly. "Put the cup down, Mrs. Hicks. I've something difficult to work out, so don't disturb me till my dinner-time."

Mrs. Hicks went out, offended, and shut the door loudly. Goon called her as she went down the passage.

"Hey, Mrs. Hicks. Half a minute. I want to ask you a question."

Mrs. Hicks came back, still looking offended. "And what might you be wanting to know?" she said.

"That butcher-boy – what was he like?" asked Goon, still vainly hoping he might have been Fatty in disguise. "And did he really bring some meat – the meat you ordered?"

"Of course he did!" said Mr. Hicks. "Two very nice lean chops, sir, the kind you like. I told you before. And I told you I didn't *see* the butcher-boy, I was upstairs. But it was him all right. I know his whistle. And I heard him calling over the fence to the next-door kid. It was Charlie Jones all right. What's all the mystery, sir?"

"Nothing, nothing, nothing!" said Mr. Goon, feeling very down-hearted. It couldn't have been Fatty after all; it *must* have been the real butcher-boy. He might have guessed that, when Mrs. Hicks told him that his chops had come. Fatty wouldn't have known that chops were ordered. Oh, what an ass he had been!

He caught sight of the note on his desk. Same square, cheap envelope. Same pasted-on bit of paper, with "Mr. goon" on, in cut-out letters. What was inside this time?

He slit the envelope open. He paused before he took out the note. He remembered what Pip had said about finger-prints. There *might* be some on the writing-paper inside. Goon fetched his own gloves and put them on. They were thick leather ones, and he found it very difficult to get the thin sheet of paper out of the envelope, while wearing such bulky gloves.

At last it was out, and he unfolded it to read. He saw the usual cut-out words and letters, all pasted on a strip of paper, which itself was stuck on the sheet of writing-paper.

"Why don't you do what you are told, egg-head", he read, and grew crimson in the face. WHO was writing these rude notes? Just wait till he got his hands on him!

He forgot all about his cup of tea, and it grew cold. Poor Goon. He simply could *not* make up his mind what to do! Why, oh why had he gone to see Fatty that morning, and left behind all the other notes?

"I can't go and report things to the Super now," he thought. "If I do, I'll have to tell him I went and told everything to that Trotteville boy – and he'll telephone to him and tell *him* to take over. He's always in the middle of things, that boy – always doing me down. What am I to do?"

Goon sat and worried for a long time. If only he could catch whoever it was delivering these notes! That would be the thing to do! He would soon solve everything then, once he got his hands on the fellow! Yes, that was certainly the thing to do. But how could he watch for him every minute of the day? It was impossible.

Then a sudden thought came to him, and he brightened. What about his nephew Ern? What about asking him to stay with him for a while, and give some pocket-money to keep a watch for him? Ern was smart.

Leaving his cold tea, he went out to Mrs. Hicks, who was sitting down enjoying her second cup of tea.

"I've got to go out," he said. "Be back by tea-time. Keep a look-out in case anyone else comes with a note."

"But your chops, sir," began Mrs. Hicks. It was no good – Goon was off on his bicycle, riding at top speed to Ern's home. Mrs. Hicks sighed and poured herself out a third cup of tea. Well, if he wasn't back by dinner-time she would have those chops herself!

Meantime Fatty and the others had been busy dis-cussing what seemed like a new, and rather sudden, mys-tery. They were in the middle of it when Mrs. Trotteville came home from her shopping, hoping to find that all the jumble had been taken from the attics, and neatly stacked into the garage. She was not very pleased to find so little done.

"Well! You said you could get everything downstairs for me by the time I came back, so that I could look over it," she said. "Whatever have you been doing?"

Nobody said a world about Mr. Goon's visit. Mrs. Trotteville was always displeased if she thought that Fatty had been "meddling in mysteries" again. She was tired of Mr. Goon coming along with complaints of his doings.

"Sorry, Mother! We'll finish everything this after-noon," said Fatty. "Larry and the rest can easily come along again. Anyway, we've got quite a few things out in the garage already."

"I should hope so!" said his mother. "I've got to look over everything, mend what can be mended, and price each thing. And by the way, Frederick, I've the names and addresses of a few people in Peterswood who have said that they will be pleased to give some jumble for the sale, if you go and collect it on a barrow."

"A *barrow*!" said Fatty. "Do you mean I'm to borrow the gardener's old barrow and trundle it through the streets? No, thank you!"

"I've arranged with the builder to lend you *his* bar-row," said his mother. "Well, I suppose it's a handcart, really, not a barrow. Larry can go with you to help you. It's for a good cause, so you can do your bit, surely."

"You have an awful lot of good causes, Mother," said Fatty. "Still, I'd rather have a mother with too many, than one with none at all! All right – I'll do some

21

collecting round and about for you. Larry and Pip can both help me."

"We'll come this afternoon and clear out the attics properly," promised Larry. "What time? Half-past two?"

"Yes," said Fatty. "And I vote we all go out to tea at the best tea-shop in the village. We'll be hungry after our hard work."

"Well, I'll pay for a good tea," said his mother, laughing. "I see you've forgotten that you want to take off some of your fat, Frederick."

"Don't remind me of that, Mother, just when I'm looking forward to meringues and chocolate éclairs," groaned Fatty.

That afternoon the five, with Buster continually getting in their way at awkward moments, carried down an enormous amount of jumble from the big attic – and just as they were in the very middle of it, a piercing whistle was heard coming up the attic stairs.

"Whoever's that?" said Fatty, startled. He looked down the steep little flight of stairs. "Gosh! It's ERN! Ern, what on earth are you doing here?"

"Come on down," said Ern. "I got something to tell you. I'm staying with my uncle – he fetched me this morning."

"Staying with *Goon*!" said Fatty, disbelievingly. "But you detest him! Half a mo – we'll all be down and hear what you've got to say. My word, Ern – this *is* a surprise! We'll be down in a tick."

Ern's New Job

Everyone was amazed to hear that Ern had suddenly come to stay with Mr. Goon. They hurried down the attic stairs at top speed. Ern was delighted to see them.

"Well," said Fatty, clapping the boy on the back. "Still the same old Ern!"

And, indeed, Ern looked exactly the same as he had always looked, though he had grown a little. He was still rather plump, and his cheeks were as brilliant red as ever. His eyes bulged a little, just like his uncle's. He grinned happily at everyone.

"Coo! You're all here. That's a bit of luck," he said.

"Let's go down to my shed," said Fatty. "We can talk without being heard there. Do you think we've got enough stuff out of the attic to satisfy my mother? The garage will soon be so full that it won't take Dad's car!"

"Yes, we've done enough," said Larry, who was feeling really tired after carrying so many heavy, awkward articles down the steep attic stairs. "I want a rest."

So off they all went, out of the side door, down the garden path, to Fatty's secluded little shed at the bottom of the garden, well-hidden among shrubs and trees.

The winter afternoon was now getting dark, and Fatty lighted a lantern, and also an oil stove, for the shed felt very chilly. Soon the glow spread over the six children and Buster, as they sat together, glad of a rest after so much hard work.

"I won't offer anyone anything to eat," said Fatty, "because we're all going out to tea, Ern – and my mother's paying, so we can have what we like. You can come with us."

"Coo!" said Ern, delighted. "Thanks a lot."

"What's all this about your uncle asking you to stay with him so suddenly?" asked Fatty.

"Well, I was just eating my dinner with Mum and my twin brothers, Sid and Perce, when my uncle comes sailing up on his bicycle," began Ern, thoroughly enjoying all the attention he was getting. "And Mum says, 'Look who's here!' And we looked, and it was Uncle Theophilus . . ."

"Oh! I'd forgotten that was Mr. Goon's name," said Bets, with a squeal of delight.

"Well, Sid and Perce, they bolted upstairs straight-away," said Ern. "They're scared stiff of Uncle because he's a policeman – and I was going, too, when Uncle yelled at me and said, 'You stay here, young Ern. I got a job for you to do. I want you to help the law'."

"Go on, Ern," said Fatty, enjoying the way Ern imitated Goon.

"Well, Uncle was sort of pally and slapped me on the back, and said, 'Well, how's the smart boy of the family,' and that made me and Mum proper suspicious," said Ern. "And then he said he wanted me to come and stay with him, and do a bit of snooping around for him – and I was going to say No, that I wouldn't, straight off like that – when he said he'd pay me proper wages!"

"Did he, now?" said Fatty. "What did he offer you?"

"Half a crown a day!" said Ern. "Loveaduck, I've never had so much money in my life! But I was smart, I was. I said, 'Done, Uncle – if you throw in an ice-cream a day as well!' And he said 'Right – if you come along with me now'."

"So you came?" said Bets. "Did your mother mind?"

"Oooh no – she's glad to get rid of one or other of us for a few days," said Ern. "She just said, 'What sort of a job is this?' And my uncle said, 'Can't tell you – it's secret. But Ern here's smart, and he'll be able to do it all right.' Coo – I never knew my uncle thought so much of me."

"I hope he'll be kind to you," said Daisy, remembering how unkind Goon had been to the boy on other occasions when he had stayed with him.

"Well, I've told him straight, I'll go back home if the job don't please me," said Ern, boastfully. "Job! Funny business it is, really. It's just to keep a look-out for anyone snooping about the house, hiding notes anywhere, when Uncle's out and can't keep watch himself. And if I do see anyone and describe him good and proper, I'm to get an extra five shillings."

"So Goon has made up his mind I'm *not* the guilty one!" said Fatty. "Did he tell you anything else, Ern?"

"No," said Ern. "But he said I could skip along here this afternoon, and you'd tell me anything you wanted to – and I was to say he'd made a mistake. He says you can burn those notes he left, and don't you bother about them any more. He can manage all right."

"He thinks we'll give up solving the mystery of the notes, I suppose," said Pip. "Well, we shan't, shall we, Fatty?"

"No," said Fatty. "There certainly is something decidedly queer about those notes. We won't burn them. We'll hang on to them. I vote we have a meeting down here tomorrow morning, and consider them carefully."

"Can I have a look at them?" asked Ern, filled with curiosity.

"They're indoors," said Fatty. "Anyway, it's almost time we went out to have our tea. Got your bike, Ern?"

"You bet," said Ern. "I say, it's a bit of good luck for me, isn't it – getting so much money! I can stand you all ice-creams in a day or two – pay you back a bit for the ones you've bought me so many times."

He grinned round at the five children, and they smiled back pleased with his good-natured suggestion. That was so like Ern.

"How are Sid and Perce, your two brothers?" asked Pip. "Does Sid still suck that awful toffee?"

"No. He's on to chewing-gum now," said Ern, seriously. "He got into trouble at school over that toffee – couldn't spit it out soon enough when the teacher got on to him about it. So now he buys chewing-gum. It's easier to manage, he says. Perce is all right too. You should have seen him and Sid scoot upstairs when Uncle arrived this morning. Atom-bombs couldn't have got them up quicker!"

They all laughed. Fatty stood up. "Well, let's go," he

said. "Ern, if your uncle is at home tomorrow morning, you come and join our meeting. You may as well listen to our plans, seeing you're more or less in this affair too."

"Oooh, I'd love to," said Ern overjoyed. "I might bring my latest pome to read to you. It's not quite finished, but I'll try and think of the ending tonight."

Everyone smiled. Ern and his poems! He did try so hard to write them, but nearly always got stuck in the middle. They all went out of Fatty's shed, and he locked it behind him carefully. No grown-up was allowed to see what treasures he had there! All his many disguises. His make-up. His false teeth and moustaches and whiskers. Mr. Goon's eyes would have fallen out of his head if he had seen them.

They lighted their bicycle lamps and rode off to the tea-shop, Buster in Fatty's bicycle basket. They left their bicycles outside the shop, and went in, Buster keeping close to heel. "A table for six, please," said Fatty, politely.

Soon they were all sitting down enjoying a truly marvellous tea. Fatty's mother had handed out ten shillings as a reward for their hard work, and that bought a very fine tea indeed – but wasn't quite enough to pay for ice-creams each as well, so Fatty delved into his own pocket as usual.

"I vote for scones and honey to begin with, macaroons to follow, and either éclairs or meringues after that, with ice-creams to end with," suggested Fatty.

"Loveaduck!" said Ern, overcome. "I wish I hadn't eaten so much dinner. What about Buster?"

"Oh, Buster can have his usual tit-bits," said Fatty, and gave the order to a most amused waitress.

"Are you sure that all this will be *enough*?" she said, smiling.

"Well, no, I'm not quite sure," said Fatty. "But that will do to start with!"

It was a hilarious meal, and Ern made them all laugh

26

till they cried by telling them of Sid's mistake over his chewing-gum the day before.

"You see, Perce had got out his clay-modelling set," began Ern, "and he was flattening out some of the clay to work it up properly, like. And Mum called him, and off he went. Then Sid came in, and what does Sid think but that them flat pieces is some of his chewing-gum! So into his mouth they went. He didn't half complain about the taste – said he'd take it back to the shop – but he wouldn't spit it out, he said he couldn't waste it. And then Perce came back, and there was an awful shindy because Sid was chewing up his bits of clay!"

Everyone roared with laughter at Ern's peculiar story. "Quite revolting," said Fatty. "Simply horrible. But very funny, the way you tell it, Ern. Don't, for pity's sake, repeat the story in front of my mother, will you?"

"I'd never *dare* to open my mouth to your mother," said Ern, looking quite scared at the thought of telling a story about Sid and Perce to Mrs. Trotteville. "Coo – even my uncle's scared of your mother, Fatty. What's the time? I've got to get back to my job sharp on half-past five, because Uncle's going out then."

"Well, you'd better scoot off," said Fatty, looking at his watch. "When you're paid to do a job, young Ern, it's better to give a few minutes more to it, than a few minutes less. That's one of the differences between doing a job honestly, and doing it dishonestly! See?"

"Right-o, Fatty," said Ern, slipping out of his chair. "I'll do anything you say. So long! See you tomorrow if I can."

"Good old Ern," said Pip, watching the boy make his way to the door of the tea-shop. "I hope old Goon will treat him all right. And if he doesn't pay him as he promised, *we'll* have something to say about that!"

"Can anyone eat any more?" said Fatty. "No? Sorry, Buster, but everyone says no, so it's no use wagging your tail like that! Well, I feel decidedly better now, if rather plumper. If *only* I could get thinner! I'll have to try some cross-country racing again."

"What! In this cold weather!" said Pip. "It would make you so hungry, you'd eat twice as much as usual – so what would be the good?"

"I hoped you'd say that, Pip, old thing," said Fatty, with a chuckle. "Well, we'll get home. Tomorrow at half-past ten, all of you. I've got a little job to do to-night, before I go to bed."

"What's that?" asked the others.

"I'm going to use my finger-printing powder, and see if I can find any unusual prints on the sheets of paper those messages were pasted on," said Fatty.

And so, all by himself in his shed, Fatty tested the sheets for strange finger-prints, feeling very professional indeed. But it was no use – the sheets were such a mass of prints, that it would have been quite impossible to decipher a strange one!

"There are Goon's prints – and all of ours," groaned Fatty. "I do hope Goon doesn't mess up any new notes. He *ought* to test for prints as soon as he gets one. Well, I hope this *is* a mystery boiling up. It certainly has the smell of one!"

A Meeting—and the First Clue

Next morning Fatty was waiting for the others down in his shed. He had biscuits in a tin, and lemonade in a bottle. He also had the four notes set out in their envelopes.

Larry and Daisy were the first to arrive. "Hallo, Fatty! Solved the mystery yet?" said Daisy.

"I don't somehow think it's going to be very easy," said Fatty. "That box is for you to sit on, Daisy. I've put a cushion on it – and there's a cushion for Bets too."

Pip and Bets arrived almost immediately, and then Ern came running down the path. Buster greeted him loudly, leaping round his ankles. He liked Ern.

"Hallo, everybody," said Ern, panting. "Am I late? I thought I wouldn't be able to come, but Uncle said he'd be in all morning, so here I am. I'm on duty this afternoon."

"Has he paid you anything yet?" asked Bets.

"No. He says he'll pay me each dinner-time," said Ern. "I asked him for a bit in advance, but he wouldn't give me any. If he had I'd have bought some sweets and brought them along for us all, but I'll do that tomorrow."

"Thanks, Ern," said Fatty. "Tell us – did you have any luck in seeing anyone snooping around, placing notes anywhere?"

"No. No luck at all," said Ern. "Uncle's quite disappointed there's no more notes. I watched him testing the one he got yesterday morning for finger-prints. All that powder and stuff! Beats me how it fetches up finger-prints!"

"Oh! Did Goon test for finger-prints too?" said Fatty, interested. "Did he find any? The note he had wouldn't have any prints of ours on it – it would show up a strange print at once."

"Well, it didn't show *anything*," said Ern. "Not a thing. Uncle said the writer must have worn gloves. Didn't mean to be found out, did he?"

"No, he didn't," said Fatty, looking thoughtful. "It rather looks as if he was afraid that his finger-prints would be recognized . . ."

"And *that* would mean that he'd had them taken already for some reason," said Larry, at once. "So he might be a bad lot – might have been in prison."

"Yes, that's true," said Fatty. "I wonder if the man who writes the notes is the one who's putting them all about Goon's garden. No wonder Goon wants to spot him, if so."

"Coo," said Ern, looking startled. "Do you think he might be dangerous? Do you think he'd shoot me if he saw me spying for him?"

"Oh no – I shouldn't think so!" said Fatty. "I don't think you *will* spot him, Ern. He'd be very careful indeed. I wish I knew what he meant by these notes, though. And why does he got to so much trouble cutting out letters and words from the newspapers, and putting them laboriously on strips of paper, and then sticking the strips on writing-paper. Why couldn't he just disguise his writing? It's easy enough to do!"

"It might be easy for you, Fatty, but not for most people," said Daisy.

"You say you saw and heard nothing at all to make you think anyone was around, and that no note was found this morning?" said Fatty to Ern. "I wonder if that was because you were there? Who is in the house when Goon is out?"

"Only Mrs. Hicks, the woman who comes in to clean," said Ern. "She's not there all the time, anyway. And I don't believe she'd notice anyone around unless they rang the bell or banged on the knocker. Why, she never even noticed the boy next door when he hopped over the fence to get his ball."

"The boy next door? Did *he* come over?" said Fatty, at once. "It's possible someone might pay him to slip the notes here and there."

"Well, I watched him like anything," said Ern. "I was peeping out of the bedroom window, see – and I saw two kids playing ball next door – and suddenly their ball came over the fence. And then the boy climbed over, got his ball and went back, looking all round in case my uncle came rushing out. He didn't have any note – he just picked up his ball and ran for his life."

"He doesn't *sound* suspicious," said Fatty, and the others nodded in agreement. "Still – you've got to suspect *any*one who comes, Ern."

"Right-o. I'll even give the next door cat the once-over if he comes," said Ern, grinning.

"Now let's consider these notes carefully," said Fatty, and spread them out in a row on the table. "I'll read them all out again. Listen, everyone, you too, Ern, because you haven't heard them before."

Fatty picked up the first one. "Number one – 'Ask Smith what his real name is'. Number two – 'Turn him out of the Ivies'. Number three – 'Call yourself a policeman? Go and see Smith!' Number four – 'You'll be sorry if you *don't* go and see Smith'."

"And I can tell you Number five," said Ern, eagerly. "It was on Uncle's desk when he was doing the fingerprint test, and I saw it. It said, 'Why don't you do what you're told, egghead?' "

Everyone laughed. Ern grinned. "Uncle didn't like that," he said.

"Well," said Fatty, "what does anyone gather from these notes?"

"There's a house called The Ivies somewhere," said Bets.

"And a man called Smith lives in it," said Daisy.

"And it's not his real name, it's a false one," said Larry.

"And if he's using a false name there must be some reason for it," added Pip, "and possibly it means that at one time or another he's been in trouble – and doesn't want people to know his real name now."

"But why should the writer of these notes want him turned out of the Ivies?" said Fatty, frowning. "And what reason would there *be* to turn him out? Well – until we find the Ivies, it's impossible to do anything. To find a house called The Ivies must be our very first step."

"I suppose we can't find the writer of the notes, can we?" suggested Daisy. "It might be a help if we knew who *he* was!"

"How can we?" asked Larry. "He doesn't give a thing away, not a thing – not his handwriting, not his finger-prints, nothing! He's so jolly careful that he's spent ages and ages snipping printed letters or words out of newspapers and pasting them on the sheet!"

"I wonder if we could find anything out about him from these little snippings," said Fatty, gazing at them. "Newspapers are printed on both sides. There might be a guide to us in something on the *other* side of the snippings. I rather think the man is using only *one* newspaper. The letters all seem to be the same type of printing."

"But goodness me – we can't *un*paste the letters from the sheets," said Bets.

"I could," said Fatty. "It would be a very tricky job, but I think I could. I've got some special stuff somewhere for that very purpose, but I've never yet used it. I'd forgotten about it. I might be able to do something tonight. It's worth trying, anyhow."

"Yes. And surely we *ought* to be able to find the house called The Ivies?" said Daisy.

"I've looked in the street directory and examined the names there of every house in Peterswood, and I'm sure Goon has too," said Fatty, gloomily. "There isn't a single one called 'The Ivies', not a single one."

"What about Marlow?" said Daisy. "There might be a house called 'The Ivies' there."

"There might. And there might be one in Maidenhead and one in Taplow," said Fatty. "But it would take absolutely ages to look up all the houses in the directory."

"What a pity the man took the name of Smith – the man who apparently lives at The Ivies," said Pip. "There are so many Smiths."

"Yes. I looked them up in the telephone directory to start with," said Fatty. "There are dozens there – and this man may not even be on the telephone. We can't go ringing up all the Smiths in the neighbourhood to find out if any of them have a false name!"

"No. Of course not," said Pip.

"Well, I simply do not see how we can even make a start," said Larry. "Have you any ideas, Fatty?"

"None," said Fatty. "Ern – what about you?"

Ern looked startled. "Well – if *you* haven't got any ideas, 'tisn't likely I would," he said. "You're the cleverest of us all, Fatty, you know you are."

"Let's have a biscuit and some lemonade," said Fatty. "And Ern – what about that poem of yours? Did you bring it along?"

"Er – well, yes, I did," said Ern, blushing, and dived into deep recesses of his clothing. He brought out a little black notebook, and opened it.

"Read away," said Fatty, handing round the biscuits. "We're waiting, Ern."

So Ern, looking very serious, read out his newest "Pome" as he called it.

" 'THE OLD OLD HOUSE

by Ern Goon

*There was a poor old house
That once was full of folk, ...
But now was sad and empty,
And to me it spoke.
It said, 'They all have left me,
The rooms are cold and bare,
The front door's locked and bolted ...' "*

Ern stopped, and looked at the others. "Well, go on, Ern – it's very good," said Fatty, encouragingly.

"I'm stuck there," said Ern, looking miserable. "It took me six months to write those lines – and now I can't go on. I suppose you can't help me, Fatty? You're so good at making up poetry."

Fatty laughed. "Yes – I can tell you how your poem goes on, Ern. Here, let me read what you've written –

and when I come to the end of it, I'll let my tongue go loose, and maybe we'll see what the end of the verse is. Here goes!"

And Fatty began to read Ern's poem out again. He didn't stop when he came to where Ern had finished. No – he went straight on, just as though he was reading more and more lines! No wonder Ern stared in the greatest astonishment!

> "There was a poor old house
> That once was full of folk,
> But now was sad and empty,
> And to me it spoke.
> It said, 'They all have fled,
> My rooms are cold and bare,
> The front door's locked and bolted,
> And all the windows stare.
> No smoke comes from my chimneys,
> No rose grows up my wall,
> But only ivy shrouds me,
> In green and shining shawl!
> No postman brings me letters,
> No name is on my gate,
> I once was called The Ivies,
> But now I'm out of date,
> The garden's poor and weedy,
> The trees won't leaf again,
> But though I fall to ruin,
> The ivy – will – remain!"

There was a silence after this. Everyone stared at Fatty in astonishment and admiration. Ern hadn't a word to say. He sat open-mouthed. How DID Fatty do it? He, Ern, had slaved for six months over the first few lines – and then Fatty had stood up and recited the rest. Without even THINKING! And Ern sorrowfully confessed to himself that Fatty's lines were much better than his.

He found his tongue at last. "Well, it's what I thought.

You're a genius, Fatty, and I'm not. That's your pome, not mine."

"No, Ern. It's yours. You *began* it, and I expect that's how it was meant to go,'' said Fatty, smiling. "I shouldn't have been able to think of the ending, if you hadn't thought of the beginning."

"It beats me. It really does," said Ern. "I say – fancy you putting in that bit about The Ivies, too – and the ivy growing up the wall. Well – even if it had no name on the gate, like you said, anyone would know it was still The Ivies, because of its 'green and shining shawl' – that's a lovely line, Fatty. You're a real poet, you are."

But Fatty wasn't listening to Ern's last few words. He stood still, staring into space, and Bets felt quite alarmed. Was Fatty ill?

"What's the matter, Fatty?" she said.

"Well – don't you *see*?" said Fatty, coming to himself again. "What I said in the verses – even if there's no name on the gate, even if the house hasn't *got* a name, it must still have got the *ivy* that gave it its old name. Why don't we go out and look for a house *covered with ivy*? We can easily cycle all round and about. We might find the very house we want!"

"Loveaduck!" said Ern, in awe. "You're a One, Fatty. You really are. You make up a pome – and it gives us the first clue! I never knew anyone like you – honest I didn't!"

Looking for Ivy!

The six children began to talk about Fatty's sudden brain-wave. Of course! Any house once called "The Ivies" must certainly be covered with ivy, or there would be no point in giving it such a name!

"But why wouldn't it *still* be called 'The Ivies'?" asked Daisy.

"It's an old-fashioned sort of name," said Larry. "Maybe it's owned now by someone who just prefers a number for their house. Some people do. The house opposite ours used to be called 'Four Towers' but now it's simply 'Number Seventeen' with the 'seventeen' written out in full."

"I think you're probably right, Larry," said Fatty. "Well, the thing to do is to go round looking for houses covered with ivy. I don't imagine that anyone would have the ivy pulled up, if they bought the house, because it clings to the wall so tightly, and sends its tiny rootlets into every nook and cranny. The ivy will still be there."

"A green and shining shawl," quoted Ern, who still hadn't recovered from Fatty's ending to his poem. "Coo, Fatty, you're a wonder! To think of you standing up there, and . . ."

"Forget it, Ern," said Fatty. "You could do it too if you let your tongue just go loose. Practice is all you need. Now, let's go on with the discussion. We're all agreed, then, that the next thing to do is to search for an ivy-covered house, with just a number, since we know there isn't a single house in Peterswood called 'The Ivies'."

"It might have another *name*," said Bets.

"Yes – you're right, Bets," said Fatty. "It might. The people who called it 'The Ivies' might not be there now. They might have moved."

"Still, we know that people called Smith live there – if what those peculiar notes say is true," said Daisy.

"So, whenever we find a house covered with ivy, we have to try and find out if the people in it are called Smith," said Larry, triumphantly. "I really feel as if we're getting somewhere now."

"I bet my uncle won't think up anything as clever as this," said Ern, thoroughly enjoying himself.

"He didn't hear Fatty's verses," said Pip. "If we hadn't heard them either, we'd not have thought of that clue – looking for an ivy-covered house that wasn't *called* "The

Ivies'. Fatty, when can we go and look for this house?"

"No time like the present," said Fatty. "Got your bike, young Ern? Then you can come with us."

"Suppose my uncle asks me what I've been up to this morning?" said Ern. "Shall I tell him I haven't seen you?"

"Certainly *not*," said Fatty, shocked. "Any fibs of that sort from you, Ern, and you don't come to any more meetings. You ought to know by now what we think of people who don't tell the truth."

"I'm sorry, Fatty," said Ern, humbly. "But I just didn't want to give anything away. My uncle's bound to ask me to tell him everything we said – and I don't want him to worm things out of me. I just thought it would make it easy, like, to say I hadn't seen you."

"Never you take the easy way out if it means being dishonest or untruthful," said Fatty. "You've got a lot of things to learn, young Ern, and that's one of them."

"I'll do anything you say, Fatty," said Ern. "Am I to tell Uncle what we've decided then?"

Fatty considered. "Well – I can see it's difficult for you, Ern. If you refuse to say anything, your uncle may be beastly to you. You can tell him we're all going out to look for houses covered with ivy. Let him make what he likes of that."

"But *he'll* go out and look for them too," objected Ern.

"Well, there's no law against anyone looking for ivy-covered houses," said Fatty, going out of the shed. "Come on, everyone. Let's go. Brrr! It's cold out here. Buster, are you coming?"

Buster certainly *was* coming. He tore out after the others, barking, and Fatty locked the door carefully behind them.

Soon they were all on their bicycles, and rode to the end of Fatty's lane. There they dismounted at Fatty's command.

"It would be a waste of time for us all to go together,"

37

said Fatty. "We'll go in pairs, and try to examine every road in Peterswood. Got your notebooks, everyone? As soon as you see an ivy-covered house, stop. Note if it has a name, or a number, and the street it's in. Don't bother about *new* houses anywhere – ivy takes years to grow. We must look out for an old house. Bets and I will go this way – you others decide which street *you'll* explore."

Bets went off with Fatty, Ern cycled away with Pip, and Daisy and Larry rode off together. "Meet at this corner in an hour's time!" yelled Fatty, as they parted.

Fatty and Bets rode slowly up the first road. "You examine the houses on one side of the road, and I'll watch the ones on the other," said Fatty.

They cycled along together, but to their disappointment not one house had any ivy at all growing up the walls. They turned down another road, and Bets suddenly gave an exclamation. "Here's a house that's green from top to bottom, Fatty."

"But not with ivy, Bets, old thing," said Fatty. "That's creeper – ordinary Virginia creeper. At least, that's what our gardener calls it. Bad luck!"

Down another road, riding very slowly this time, as there were big houses here, standing right back from the road, and difficult to see because of trees in the front gardens.

"Here's one covered with ivy!" said Fatty at last. "Look, Bets!"

"Yes. But it's got a name on the gate," said Bets. "See – Barton House."

"Well, we know we shan't find a house called 'The Ivies'," said Fatty, "because there's none in the directory. We'll have to put this down, Bets. Now wait while I get my notebook."

He took it from his pocket and wrote quickly, Bets peeping over his shoulder. "Barton Grange. Old house, with ivy almost up to roof. In Hollins Road."

He shut his notebook. "Good. That's one ivy-covered

38

house, anyway. I wonder if anyone called Smith lives there. We'll have to find out."

They only found one more ivy-covered house and that was quite a small one, in Jordans Road. It had obviously once been a cottage belonging to the big house nearby, but had been sold, and now had its own little garden, and a hedge round it.

"What's it called?" said Fatty. "Oh – it hasn't a name – just a number. Number 29, Jordans Road. It looks well-kept – nice curtains at the windows, neat garden. I say, Bets – what about going to ask if people called Smith live here? You just never know your luck!"

"You go, Fatty," said Bets, who was always shy of strange people.

"Right," said Fatty, and leaned his bicycle against the trim little hedge. With Buster at his heels he went in at the gate. "I bet someone called Cholmondley or Montague-Paget lives here," he thought, "just when I'm looking for a nice short, straightforward Smith!"

He rang the brightly-polished bell. At once a dog began to bark inside the house, and Buster stiffened. Fatty picked him up immediately. He didn't want a dog-fight on the door-step!

Someone came up the passage to the front door, and it opened. At once a Pekinese flew out, dancing round excitedly, barking at the top of its voice. Buster wriggled in Fatty's arms, and began barking too.

"Come here, Ming!" said the little old woman at the door, and Ming obeyed, still barking. "What is it you want?"

"Er – I'm looking for someone called Smith," said Fatty, politely. "I don't know if you can help me."

"Smith? Well, that's *our* name," said the old lady. "Who are you? And which of us do you want – me, or my husband?"

For once in a way Fatty was taken aback. He hadn't for one moment imagined that he would find a Smith in an ivy-covered house so quickly, and he hardly knew what to say! But Fatty was never at a loss for long.

"Er – I'd like to see Miss Annabella-Mary Smith," he said. "That's if she's here, of course."

"Oh, you've got the *wrong* Smith," said the old lady, briskly. "There's no *Miss* Smith here, only a Mr. and Mrs. Smith – my husband and myself. Wait – my husband's here. He may know of another Smith somewhere near. John! Come here a minute, will you, dear?"

A nice old man appeared, with a wrinkled, kindly face, and twinkling eyes. Fatty liked him at once. His wife repeated what Fatty had said.

"Miss Annabella-Mary Smith?" he said. "No, I don't know anyone of that name in this road, anyway. We used to live in the big house next door, you know, and knew everyone in the district – but the place was too big for us and we moved into this little place – used to be our gardener's cottage, and very cosy it is too!"

"Was it ever called 'The Ivies', asked Fatty, hopefully. Mr. Smith shook his head.

"No. It was just called 'The Cottage', he said. "Sorry I can't help you."

"I'm very sorry to have bothered you," said Fatty, and he raised his cap politely, pleased to have met with such a nice old couple. He went back to Bets and told her what had happened.

"I felt rather mean, bothering such nice people," he said, putting Buster down. "Well – although their name is Smith and they live in an ivy-covered house, they can't be anything to do with the Smith in those notes. That little place used to be called 'The Cottage' not 'The Ivies'. Come along – on with the search, Bets. I wonder how the others are getting on!"

Bets and Fatty were astonished to discover that there were no more houses with ivy in the roads they rode along. "Ivy must have gone out of fashion," said Bets. "There are plenty of houses with roses on the wall, and clematis and wisteria, and creeper – but no ivy! Well – I must say ivy is a dark, rather ugly thing to cover a house with, when you can get so much prettier things to grow up the walls. What's the time, Fatty?"

"Time to meet the others," said Fatty, looking at his watch. "Come on – let's see how they've got on. Better than we have, I hope. Certainly we found an ivy-covered house, and people called smith – but not the ones we want!"

They cycled off to the corner where they were to meet the others. Larry and Daisy were there already, waiting patiently. Ern and Pip arrived soon after, Ern grinning all over his face as usual.

"Any luck?" asked Fatty.

"We're not quite sure," said Pip. "Let's got to your shed, Fatty. We can't talk here. We'll all compare notes, and see if we've got anything useful!"

Pip and Ern have some News

Soon all six, with Buster running round busily, were sitting once more in Fatty's shed. He produced some chocolate biscuits, and Buster sat up and begged at once.

'No, Buster. Think of your figure," said Fatty, solemnly. Buster barked loudly.

"He says – 'You jolly well think of *yours*, Fatty!' said Bets, with a chuckle. "I'll only have one, thank you. It's getting near dinner-time, and we're having steak and kidney pudding – I don't want not to be hungry for that!"

"Well – any news?" asked Fatty, producing his notebook.

"You tell yours first," said Pip.

"There's not much," said Fatty. "Bets and I found one big ivy-covered house called Barton Grange, in Hollins Road. Ivy almost up to the roof. We'll have to find out if it was ever called 'The Ivies'. And we found a nice little cottage, with no name in Jordans Road, No. 29 – AND the people who live there are called Smith."

Everyone sat up in surprise. "Goodess – you don't mean to say you've hit on the right house and people straightaway!" said Larry, astonished.

"No. Apparently the house once belonged to the gardener of the big place next to it, and was called 'The *Cottage*' – not 'The Ivies'," said Fatty. "And the Smiths weren't the right Smiths either. Most disappointing! We'll have to rule it out, I'm afraid. Well, what about you, Larry and Daisy?"

"Absolutely nothing to report," said Larry. "We did see one old ivy-covered house – ivy right up to the roof, so it must have been quite an old house."

"But its name was Fairlin Hall," said Daisy. "And it was empty. We rode in at the drive, because we couldn't see the house properly from the front gates. We guessed it would be empty because there was a big board up outside 'To be Sold'."

"It looked a dreadful old place," said Larry. "Old-fashioned, with great pillars at the front door, and heavy balconies jutting out everywhere. I wonder if people ever sat out on those stone balconies in the old days."

"It looked so lonely and dismal," said Daisy. "It really gave me the shivers. It reminded me of the line in that poem, Fatty – 'All my windows stare'. They did seem to stare at us, as if they were hoping we might be coming to live there, and put up curtains and light fires."

"But we ruled it out because it was called Fairlin Hall, and was *empty*," said Larry. "No Smith there!"

"Quite right," said Fatty. "What about you and Ern, Pip?"

"We found *two* ivy-covered houses," said Pip. "And one really might be worth while looking into, Fatty. Ern and I agreed that it *might* be the one!"

"Ah – this is better news," said Fatty. "Out with it, Pip."

"Well, Ern found the first one," said Pip, seeing that Ern had taken out his notebook, and was looking hopefully at him, eager to enter into the debate.

"It was called 'Dean Lodge', and was in Bolton Road," said Ern, in a very business-like voice, flicking over the pages of his notebook, as he had seen his uncle do. "Ivy-covered to the roof – well, almost to the roof. And it wasn't empty, like the one Pip talked about. It had people in it."

"Called Smith?" said Bets.

"No. Afraid not," said Ern, looking hard at his notebook if he needed to refer to a list of names. "Me and Pip decided it might be a likely place, as the people who lived in it first *might* have called it 'The Ivies'. So we decided to ask if anyone called Smith lived there now."

"And was there?" asked Fatty.

"No. The milkman came up just as we were looking at it, and I asked him," said Ern. "I said, 'Anyone called Smith live here, mate?' And he said no, it was the Willoughby-Jenkins, or some such name, and they'd been there sixteen years, and he'd brought them their milk every single morning on those sixteen years, except the two days he got married."

Everyone laughed at Ern's way of telling his little tale. "Now you, Pip," he said, shutting his notebook.

"Well, the house I spotted was in Haylings Lane," said Pip, referring to *his* notebook. "Not a very big one, and not very old. Actually it isn't really a house now, it's been made into half-shop, half-house, and over the front gate is a notice. It said 'Smith and Harris, Nursery-Men. Plants and shrubs for sale. Apply at house'."

"*Smith* and Harris!" said Fatty, interested at once. "And you say the house is ivy-covered?"

"Well – not exactly *covered*," said Pip. "It had a kind of variegated ivy growing half-way up the whitewashed walls, the leaves were half-yellow and half-green – rather unusual, really. We thought perhaps as Smith and Harris grew shrubs and things, they probably planted one

43

of their own ivies there, to cover the house. But the place wasn't called 'The Ivies'. It was just called 'Haylings Nursery' – after the lane, I suppose. I told you it was in Haylings Lane."

"Yes," said Fatty, thoughtfully, "I can't help thinking that your house is the most likely one, Pip. Ivy up the walls – owned by *Smith* and Harris – and it *might* have been called 'The Ivies' before they took it over."

"Well – what shall we do next?" said Ern, eagerly. "Loveaduck – whatever would my uncle say if he knew all we'd been doing this morning!"

"Let's quickly run over the ivy-covered houses we've all discovered," said Fatty, "and make up our minds which are definitely no good, and which are worth enquiring into. I'll take Bets and mine first."

He ran over them quickly. "Barton Grange, Hollins Road. Ivy-covered. Well, I suppose we'd better find out if people called Smith lived there, and if it was ever named 'The Ivies'. Then there was the house we found in Jordans Road, but we've ruled that out already, because it never *was* called The Ivies. Then there's the house called Fairlin Hall, that Larry and Daisy found – but it's empty, so that's no good."

"So that only leaves Haylings Nursery, owned by Smith and Harris," said Pip. "I vote we enquire into that! If that's no good, we'll find out a bit more about Barton Grange in Hollins Road, the one you and Bets found, Fatty."

"I wonder if my mother knows who lives in Barton Grange," said Fatty. "She's lived in Peterswood so long, she knows practically everybody. I'll ask her. Gosh, look at the time! And there's our dinner-bell! Buck up, all of you, you'll get into a row!"

"Oh my goodness!" said Ern, in a panic. "What will Uncle say if I'm late! And he's supposed to pay me my first half-crown at dinner-time. Good-bye, all!"

He raced off to get his bicycle, and Larry and the others rode away at top speed too.

44

"I'll telephone you later!" Fatty shouted after them, and ran indoors to his own lunch. How the time flew when there was detective work to be done! He washed his hands, slicked back his hair and went into the dining-room, to find his mother just about to sit down herself.

"So sorry I'm a bit late, Mother," said Fatty, sliding into his seat.

"It will be a nice surprise for me when you decide to be punctual, Frederick," said his mother. "What have you been doing this morning?"

"Oh – just messing about with the others," said Fatty, truthfully. "We did a bit of cycling. Mother, can you tell me something? Who lives at Barton Grange – the big house in Hollins Road?"

"Barton Grange – let me think now," said his mother. "First the Fords lived there – then the old man died and his widow went to live with her daughter. Then the Jenkins came there – but they lost all their money and left. Then the Georges came – now what happened to them? I know they left very hurriedly indeed – there was some trouble..."

"And then did the Smiths come?" asked Fatty, hopefully.

"The Smiths? What Smiths?" said his mother, in surprise.

"Oh – I don't really know," said Fatty. "Anyway – who's there now? It wouldn't *be* people called Smith, would it?"

"No. Nothing *like* Smith," said his mother, decidedly. "Yes – I remember now – it's old Lady Hammerlit. I don't know her at all – she's bedridden, poor old thing. But why are you so interested in Barton Grange, Frederick?"

"Well, I was – but I'm not now," said Fatty, disappointed to find that no Smiths lived there. "Mother, I suppose you don't know any place that was once called 'The Ivies', do you?"

"Frederick, what *is* all this?" asked his mother, sus-

45

piciously. "You're not getting mixed up in anything peculiar again, are you? I don't want that unpleasant Mr. Goon here again, complaining about you."

"Mother, he's got *nothing* to complain about," said Fatty, impatiently. "And you haven't answered my question. Was there ever any house called 'The Ivies' in Peterswood – its name will have been changed by now. We've heard of one – but nobody seems to know of it now."

"The Ivies?" said Mrs. Trotteville. "No – I don't think I've ever heard of it. I've lived in Peterswood for nineteen years, and as far as I remember there never *has* been any place called 'The Ivies'. Why do you want to know?"

Fatty didn't like the way his mother was questioning him. He wasn't going to tell any fibs, and yet he couldn't give away the reason for his questions, or his mother would at once complain that he was "getting mixed up in something peculiar again".

He reached out for the salt – and upset his glass of water. "Oh *Frederick*!" said his mother, vexed. "You really are careless. Dab it with your table-napkin, quick."

Fatty heaved a sigh of relief. The subject was certainly changed now! "Sorry, Mother," he said. "I say – what was that story you used to tell about the man who sat next to you at a big dinner-party one night – and told you what a big fish he had caught, and . . ."

"Oh yes," said his mother, and laughed. "He stretched out his arms to show me how big it was, and said, 'You should have *seen* the fish –' and knocked a whole dish of fish out of the waiter's hand all over himself. He certainly saw a lot of fish then!"

Clever old Fatty! No more awkward questions were asked about 'The Ivies' after that. His mother happily related a few more amusing stories, to which Fatty listened with great enjoyment. In the middle of them, the telephone bell rang.

"You answer it," said his mother. "It's probably your father to say he'll be late tonight."

But it wasn't. It was Ern, and he sounded very upset indeed.

"That you, Fatty? I say, my uncle's in an awful temper with me, because I wouldn't tell him all we did this morning. He won't pay me my wages. And he says I'm not to go home, I've got to stay here. What shall I do? Shall I scoot off home? I don't want to, because it's so nice to be in the middle of a mystery with all of you."

"I'll come up and see Mr. Goon," said Fatty, sorry for poor old Ern. "You stay put. I'll be up in half an hour's time!"

Fatty pays a call on Mr. Goon

Fatty kept his promise to Ern. As soon as he had finished his lunch, he put Buster in his bedroom and told him to stay there.

"I'm going to see your enemy, old Goon," he told Buster, "and much as you would like to go with me and snap at his ankles, I don't feel that it would be wise this afternoon, Buster. I've got to get poor old Ern his wages!"

Fatty fetched his bicycle and rode off, pondering as he went what to tell Mr. Goon. He decided to tell him everything that had happened that morning, even about Smith and Harris.

"If the Smith of Smith and Harris *is* the man written of in those notes, and he's using a false name to cover up some misdeed or other, I suppose it would sooner or later be a job for Goon to take over," Fatty thought. "He'd have to find out what the fellow had done – and why he should be turned out of 'The Ivies' – if that's the place that is now called 'Haylings Nursery'. Anyway, I can't let poor old Ern get into trouble."

He arrived at Goon's house, and knocked vigorously at the door. Mrs. Hicks arrived in her usual breathless manner.

"There now!" she said. "I've just bin reading the tea-leaves in my after-dinner cup of tea – and they *said* there would be a stranger coming to the house!"

"How remarkable," said Fatty, politely. "Tell Mr. Goon that Frederick Trotteville wishes to see him, please."

Mrs. Hicks left him standing in the hall, and went into the policeman's office. He scowled at her. "Bring that boy in," he said, before she could speak. "I saw him through the window. I've got something to SAY to him!"

Fatty walked in and nodded to Mr. Goon. He knew that the policeman would not ask him to sit down, so he sat down at once, without being asked. He wasn't going to stand in front of Mr. Goon like a schoolboy called in for a talking-to!

"Ah, Mr. Goon," he said, in an amiable voice. "I felt I should like to see you for a few minutes. About Ern."

"Ern! I'm *tired* of Ern!" said Mr. Goon. "Thinks he can come here and eat me out of house and home, go out when he wants to, solve mysteries, and cheek me into the bargain, *and* expects me to pay him for all that!"

"But didn't you promise to pay him?" asked Fatty, in a surprised voice. "I must say that Ern has done very well, so far. Where is he?"

"Upstairs. Locked into his room," said Mr. Goon, in a surly voice. "And I'd like to tell you this, Master Frederick Trotteville – I haven't time to waste on you. I've business to do this afternoon, see?"

"Right, Mr. Goon," said Fatty, standing up at once. "I only came to tell you what Ern and the rest of us had been doing this morning. I thought you'd like to know."

"But that's what I *asked* Ern! And all he said was that you'd gone hunting for houses covered with ivy!" said

48

Mr. Goon, almost exploding with wrath. "Telling me tales like that! Making fun of me! I ticked him off properly for telling me untruths. Then he had the cheek to ask me for half a crown!"

Fatty looked sternly at Mr. Goon. "Ern was quite right, Mr. Goon. He told you the absolute truth. We *did* go searching for ivy-covered houses – and if you were half as cute as that young nephew of yours, you'd guess at once *why* we decided to do such a thing."

Mr. Goon stared at Fatty in surprise. Ern had told him the truth, had he? But why go after ivy-covered houses? Then it all dawned on poor Mr. Goon at once. Of course – they were looking for houses that *might* have been called "The Ivies" at some time or another! Why hadn't *he* thought of that?

"Well, I'll go now," said Fatty, politely. "I shouldn't punish Ern, Mr. Goon. He was telling you the truth. But obviously you don't want to hear any more about the matter, so I'll go."

"No! No, sit down," almost shouted Mr. Goon. "You tell me about these here ivy-covered houses."

"I wouldn't dream of holding up your work," said Fatty, and began to walk out of the room.

Mr. Goon knew when he was beaten. "Here! You come back, Master Frederick," he called. "I've made a mistake, I see it all now. I'd like to hear anything you've got to say."

"Fetch Ern down, then," said Fatty. "He's in on this. He did some very good work this morning. You ought to be proud of Ern, not disbelieve him, and lock him up and refuse to pay him. The work he did this morning was worth a lot !"

Mr. Goon began to wonder if he had made a great mistake about Ern. According to Fatty Ern was much cleverer than he had thought him. Oh, Ern *could* be smart, – he knew that – but to hear this boy Frederick Trottville talking about him, you'd think Ern was really *brainy*.

49

"Well – I'll get Ern down," he said, and got up heavily from his chair. He went upstairs and Fatty could hear him unlocking Ern's door. Ern shot out at once, dodging round his uncle as if he expected a cuff. He came down the stairs two at a time, and ran into the office.

"I heard your voice, Fatty!" he said, gladly. "Coo – you're a real brick to come. How did you make my uncle let me out?"

"Listen, Ern – I'm going to tell him quite shortly about this morning," said Fatty, quickly, hearing Mr. Goon treading heavily down the stairs. "But I want you to tell him about the house that you and Pip discovered – Haylings Nursery, run by Smith and Harris, see? I've decided that he'd better know about it."

Ern just had time to nod before Mr. Goon came into the room. He sat down and cleared his throat.

"Well," he said, "I hear that the tale you told me wasn't far off the mark, young Ern. If you'd told me a bit more, I'd have listened."

"But you *wouldn't* listen, Uncle," said Ern. "You just roared at me when I asked for my half-crown, and rushed me upstairs and . . ."

"Well, I'm sure your uncle is quite willing to pay you now," said Fatty. "I've told him you were a great help this morning. In fact I think he should pay you five shillings, not half a crown. You and Pip were the most successful of us all."

"Here! I'm not paying Ern any five shillings," said Mr. Goon at once.

"In that case I shall not say any more," said Fatty, and stood up. "You've been unfair to Ern, Mr. Goon, and I should have thought you'd have liked to make it up to him a bit. My word, he did some good work this morning. He and Pip may have put us on to the track of Mr. Smith."

"What! The Smith mentioned in those notes?" said Goon astonished.

Fatty nodded. "Maybe. We don't know for certain,

of course. You'll be able to judge if you hear what Ern has to say. But as I consider the information is worth five shillings, I shan't give Ern permission to tell you unless you pay him – and pay him now, in front of me."

Ern's rather bulging eyes bulged even more when he heard Fatty talking to his dreaded uncle in such a cool, determined voice. He gazed at Fatty in awe and admiration. What a friend to have!

Mr. Goon's eyes bulged too – not with admiration, but with wrath and annoyance. He glared at Ern and Fatty. But again he knew he was beaten. That toad of a boy! He was somehow always just a little bit ahead of him. Mr. Goon heaved a great sigh, and delved into his trousers pocket. Ern's eyes brightened as he heard the clink of coins.

Goon brought out two half-crowns. He put them on the table beside Ern. "Here you are," he said. "But mind – if I think you don't deserve it, back it comes!"

"You keep it for me, Fatty," said Ern, hurriedly passing it to Fatty. "So's I don't spend it all at once, see?"

Fatty laughed and pocketed the money. He didn't trust Goon any more than Ern did. "Well, now you can tell him what we did this morning, Ern," he said. "He knows that we went out hunting for ivy-covered houses – you told him that, and he didn't believe you. But he knows it's true now, and he knows *why* we went. I'll just say, Mr. Goon, that we found a fair number of ivy-covered houses, not one of them called 'The Ivies' of course, or it would be in the directory – but that we decided that the only one worth looking into was the one that Ern and Pip found together. Now you do the talking, Ern."

Ern told his story well. He described Haylings Nursery, half-shop, half-house, well covered with variegated ivy, and told about the board outside, "Smith and Harris".

"And we were going to find out if the Mr. Smith was the one mentioned in the notes," finished Ern.

"But I decided that perhaps that was *your* job, not ours, Mr. Goon," said Fatty. "If it *is* the Mr. Smith, then, according to the notes, it's a false name – and you can probably easily find out what his real name is, by making a few enquiries into his past."

"H'm!" said Goon, most interested. "Yes – yes, I can. And you've been wise to come to me about this, Master Frederick. This is a job for the police, as you said. *I'll* take this over now. You keep out of it. I think there's no doubt that the Smith in 'Smith and Harris' is the man who is going under a false name – a criminal who's been in prison, probably. Well, if so, there will be a record of his finger-prints, and we'll soon find his name."

"How will you get his finger-prints?" asked Fatty, with much interest.

"Oh, I have my own ways of doing that," said Goon, putting on a very cunning expression, which Fatty didn't like at all.

"Well – it isn't by any means certain that this fellow Smith is anything to do with those notes, you know," said Fatty, getting up. "Better be a bit careful, in case he isn't, Mr. Goon."

"You don't need to give *me* any instructions," said Goon, annoyed. "I've been in the police force long enough to know my way about."

Fatty said good-bye and went. Ern was told to go and keep his usual watch from his bedroom window, in case anyone turned up with another note. Goon finished some reports and then decided to go and interview Mr. Smith of Smith and Harris. Ha – good thing that fat boy had had the sense to tell him about it. And fancy young Ern discovering the house! Goon brooded for a while over the five shillings he had parted with.

"Good mind to go and get it off him," he thought. "No, I can't – he's given it to that fat boy. Well – I'd better get down to Haylings Lane, and see this Mr. Smith."

He went to get his bicycle, passing through the kitchen

where Mrs. Hicks was reading the tea-leaves in her cup again. Mr. Goon shouted.

"You and your tea-leaves!" he said. "Waste of time!"

He went out of the kitchen door and shut it with a bang. Lazy, careless woman – always breaking things, always having cups of tea, always ... Mr. Goon's thoughts stopped suddenly as he saw something that gave him a real shock.

One of those anonymous notes! Yes, it must be. It lay on the kitchen window-sill – a cheap square envelope, and on it was "Mr. goon" just as before, with a small letter for his surname. He stared at it in amazement.

Well, *Ern* must have seen who put it there – and so must Mrs. Hicks! No one could have come across the garden to the kitchen window-sill without being seen! He strode indoors with the letter.

"ERN!" he yelled. "ERN! Come down here. And you, Mrs. Hicks, you sit still. I've got a few questions to ask you both. Ho yes – I certainly have!"

Ern gets into trouble

Ern had heard his uncle's stentorian call, and leapt up, scared. *Now* what was the matter? Thank goodness he had handed that five shillings to Fatty.

He tore down the stairs, two steps at a time. "What is it, Uncle? What's the matter?"

Mrs. Hicks was sitting in her chair, looking very startled, staring at Mr. Goon.

"See here, Ern," said Mr. Goon, in a voice of thunder. "See here – another of those notes I told you about. Put on the window-sill outside the kitchen here! Mrs. Hicks! How long have you been sitting here, facing the window?"

"About three minutes," said Mrs. Hicks, looking quite taken aback. "I did my washing-up, and then sat down for my second cup of tea. Not more than three minutes ago."

"Did you see anyone come into the garden?" demanded Goon.

"Not a soul," answered Mrs. Hicks. "Well, bless us all, is that really another of them ominous letters, sir – or whatever you call them? And left on the window-sill too! What a nerve!"

"You *must* have seen someone put it there," said Goon, exasperated.

"Well, it wasn't there ten minutes ago, that I do know," said Mrs. Hicks. "Because I opened the window to throw out some bread to the birds, Mr. Goon, and I'd have noticed at once if that letter was there. I'm not blind. And don't you glare at me like that, Mr. Goon, you make me feel right down queer!"

"Well – someone must have come over the fence, crossed the garden, and actually placed the note on the sill within the last ten minutes," said Goon. "Ernie *must* have seen them, even if you didn't. Ern, did you see anyone?"

"No, no one," answered Ern, puzzled. "No one at all."

"Then you couldn't have been watching," said Goon, losing his temper.

"I *was* watching, I was sitting at my window all the time," said Ern, indignantly. "I tell you, nobody came into the yard, NOBODY!"

"Then how did this note get here?" shouted Goon. "There's Mrs. Hicks here in the kitchen, and you upstairs at the window – and yet someone steals into the yard under your very eyes, leaves the note on the sill and goes away again."

"Well, I dunno!" said Ern, bewildered. "If *I* didn't see anyone, and Mrs. Hicks didn't either, there couldn't have *been* anybody. Unless he was invisible!"

54

"Now don't you cheek me," said Mr. Goon. "Invisible indeed! I don't suppose Mrs. Hicks would see anything under her nose except tea-leaves, and . . ."

"Don't you sauce *me*!" said Mrs. Hicks, annoyed.

"And as for Ern, here, he must have been reading one of those comics of his!" said Goon. "Ern – speak the truth. YOU WEREN'T WATCHING!"

"I was, Uncle, I was," said poor Ern, retreating as his uncle came forward towards him. "I do honest work. You paid me to watch, and I do watch when I'm up there. I tell you nobody came into that garden since you sent me upstairs."

Goon aimed his hand at him, but Ern ducked and the policeman's fingers caught the edge of a table. He danced round in pain. Ern tore out of the house at top speed. He snatched up his bicycle and rode off on it. He wouldn't stay with his uncle one more hour! Disbelieving him like that! Trying to cuff him when he'd done nothing wrong! Mrs. Hicks hadn't seen anyone. Well, if *she* hadn't, how could *he* have seen anybody!

Mr. Goon tore open the square envelope, then saw Mrs. Hicks staring open-mouthed, and stamped back into his office. The note was in message-form again, made with cut-out letters as before. Goon read it. It was even more puzzling that the others.

"When you see Smith, say SECRETS to him. Then watch him show his heels."

"Gah!" said Mr. Goon, in disgust. "What's it all mean? *Secrets*, now! What secrets? All right, I'll say 'secrets' to this Mr. Smith at Haylings Nursery when I see him! I'm getting tired of this. That boy Ern! Sitting upstairs like that and letting the fellow who writes these notes come and put one on the window-sill under his very nose – and I paid him five shillings!"

He was just going out again to get his bicycle when he stopped. Hadn't he better telephone to that fat boy and say another note had arrived – and tell him how badly Ern had behaved? Right down dishonest of Ern it was, to take his five shillings, and then not do his job. And most ungrateful too.

So Goon telephoned to a rather surprised Fatty and told him about the new letter, and what it contained. Fatty noted it down at once "When you see Smith, say SECRETS to him. Then watch him show his heels."

Goon went on to tell about Ern, and how he had failed to spot anyone coming into the garden with the note. "Reading his comics, that's what he was doing, instead of paying attention to his job, as he was paid to do," grumbled Goon. "Can't let Ern get away with behaviour like that, you know – taking money for what he doesn't do. You'd better let me have that five bob back."

"Sorry, Mr. Goon, but you paid Ern for what he'd *already* done, not for what he was *going* to do," said Fatty. "That five shillings is Ern's. What are you going to do now? Go to see Smith and Harris?"

"Yes," said Goon. "But about that five bob. If Ernie comes up to you, you tell him I want half-a-crown back, see?"

Fatty put down the receiver, cutting off any more remarks from the angry Goon. He felt sorry that Ern had failed to see anyone coming into the garden with another note – in full daylight too. The messenger certainly had a nerve to do a thing like that!

He heard the sound of a bicycle bell outside in the drive and looked out of the window. It was Ern, panting with his exertions to reach Fatty's house at the first possible moment.

"Hallo, Ern," said Fatty. "Your uncle's just been on the phone. I hear there's another anonymous note – put on the window-sill under everyone's nose, apparently. How on earth was it that you didn't spot whoever brought it? Apparently it happened while you were supposed to be watching."

"I *was* watching," said Ern, indignantly. "You told me to do my job honestly, and I did. I tell you, Fatty, as

56

soon as Uncle sent me upstairs to watch, I sat at my window and glued my eyes on the yard. I did, really. I saw some bread dropping into the yard, and I guessed it was Mrs. Hicks throwing some out to the birds. She says the note wasn't on the window-sill when she threw out the bread."

"And after she threw it out, you still kept your eyes glued on the yard below?" asked Fatty, doubtfully. "Didn't Mrs. Hicks see anyone either?"

"No. No one. Well, if *she* had, I'd have seen him too, wouldn't I?" said Ern, half-angry. "She was sitting opposite the window – she could almost have reached out and touched it! Well, if *she* didn't see anyone, how could *I*? I just don't understand it, Fatty. The note *must* have been there when Mrs. Hicks threw out the bread – and she didn't see it – that's the only explanation."

"I suppose it is," said Fatty. "There's something really queer about it though, I can't just put my finger on it. Well, I expect your uncle will cool down again, Ern. You can stay here for tea though, if you like. I shouldn't think there's much point in your going back to do any more watching – there isn't likely to be another note today!"

"Oh thanks, Fatty. I'd like to stay here," said Ern. "Can I help you with anything?"

"Yes. I'm going to pack up some of the jumble to take to the Village Hall some time," said Fatty. "You can help me with that. I wonder how your uncle will get on with Smith and Harris. It's *possible* that Smith may be the man mentioned in the notes. Well, we shall soon know."

Mr. Goon was not getting on very well in his afternoon's work. In fact, he was having rather a bad time. He had arrived at the Nursery in a bad temper, owing to Ern's failure to spot the messenger who brought the last anonymous note. He rode in at the gate at top speed and almost knocked down a man coming up the path wheeling a barrow.

"Look where you're going!" shouted the man, as a

flower-pot crashed to the ground. Goon dismounted, and spoke in his most official manner.

"I want to see Smith and Harris."

"Well, you're speaking to half of them," said the man, setting the barrow legs down on the path. "I'm Harris. What do you want? I've got a licence for my dog, and one for my radio, and one for my van, and . . ."

"I haven't come about licences," said Goon, with a feeling that the man was making fun of him. "I want to see Mr. Smith."

"Oh now – that's rather difficult," said Mr. Harris, rubbing his chin, and making a rasping noise as he did so. "Yes, rather difficult."

"Is he in the house?" said Mr. Goon, impatiently. "Or out in the nursery gardens?"

"No, no. You won't find him there," said Mr. Harris, who had taken a real dislike to the bumptious policeman. "I couldn't rightly put my finger on him at the moment."

"Well, I *must* see him," said Goon. "It's important. Don't put me off, please. Take me to him."

"Oh, I haven't time to do that," said Mr. Harris. "It's too far to take you when I'm busy, like. I've only one man working for me, and time's precious."

Mr. Goon began to feel exasperated. Where was this elusive Mr. Smith? He decided to put a leading question.

"Is Mr. Smith his real name?" he asked, bluntly. Mr. Harris looked very startled indeed. He stared at Mr. Goon and rasped his rough chin again.

"Far as I know it is," he said. "Known him all my life I have, and he always went by the name of Smith, since he was a tiddler. You being funny?"

"No," said Mr. Goon, shortly, disappointed to hear that Smith's name was apparently correct. "Er – can you tell me if this place was ever called 'The Ivies'?"

"And why for should it be?" demanded Mr. Harris. "It was Haylings Nursery when I bought it, and Haylings Nursery afore that, and probably Haylings Nursery afore you were born, Mr. Nosey Policeman. What's this about The Ivies?"

"Well – you've got ivy growing up the wall," said Mr. Goon, beginning to feel very foolish, and wishing he had looked up how old the Haylings Nursery was. "Now please – I want you to show me where Mr. Smith is."

"All right. Seeing as you insist," said Mr. Harris, and leaving his barrow on the path, he took Mr. Goon indoors. He led him to a big round globe of the world, and swung it a little, so that South America came into view. Mr. Harris then pointed to a town marked there.

"See that place Rio de Janeiro? Well, *that's* where he is. Retired there twenty years ago, he did, and I carried on by myself – but I still keep the old name going – Smith and Harris. You catch the next plane there, Mister, and ask him if his name's Smith. He won't mind telling you."

And with that he burst into such a roar of laughter that Goon was almost deafened. Very angry at the joke played on him, the policeman departed, looking as dignified as he could. But right to the end of the lane he could hear Mr. Harris's delighted guffaws.

Why hadn't he let that fat boy interview Mr. Harris? It would have done him good to have that silly joke played on *him*. Policemen should be treated with more respect! Mr. Goon was Very Annoyed Indeed.

Fatty comes to a Full Stop

Mr. Goon never told anyone all that had happened at Haylings Nursery. When Fatty telephoned him that evening to ask if he had had any success, Mr. Goon said very little.

"There is no Mr. Smith there now," he said. "He left

59

the firm twenty years ago. It was a waste of my time to go there. Is Ern with you, Master Frederick?"

"Yes. I'm just sending him back to you," said Fatty. "He's been a great help to me this afternoon – nice of you to send him up, Mr. Goon. Thanks very much."

Goon was astonished. Hadn't Ern told Fatty how angry he had been with Ern, then – and that he had tried to hit him? Well, Ern could stay another night with him, and then he could go home. He wasn't much good as a watcher, and as for paying him another penny, he wasn't even going to *think* of it!

Ern arrived, wondering how Goon was going to treat him. He sent him out to have his supper with Mrs. Hicks in the kitchen. "Got some work to do," he said, and Ern fled thankfully to the warm kitchen.

He sat down by the fire, and watched Mrs. Hicks making some pastry. "Funny how neither of us saw that fellow, whoever he was, bringing that note this afternoon," said Ern.

"Well, I wasn't really looking," said Mrs. Hicks. "I was just sitting here with my teacup, reading the tea-leaves, like I always do. *You* couldn't have been looking either, young man. You can tell fibs to your uncle, if you like, but you needn't tell them to me. You just wasn't looking!"

"Oooh, I *was*," said Ern. "I tell you I never took my eyes off that yard. Never once. When I'm paid to do a thing I do it, see? And I never saw anyone – all I saw were the birds flying down to peck at the bread you threw out."

"Oh – you saw me doing that, did you?" said Mrs. Hicks. "Well, it's funny you didn't see who brought that note then, because he must have come along just after that – as I was telling your uncle."

"He *couldn't* have come then," said Ern. "I tell you I was watching all the time, Mrs. Hicks. *I'm* not making a mistake, I know I'm not."

"Are you telling me that *I* am, then?" said Mrs. Hicks,

60

looking so fierce that Ern felt quite alarmed. "You just be careful of that tongue of yours, young Ern, else not a mite of supper do you get."

Ern subsided, feeling puzzled. Everyone was cross with him just now – but on the whole it was safer to sit with Mrs. Hicks in the kitchen rather than with his uncle in the office. He wondered if Mrs. Hicks would like to hear his "pome". It might put her into a better temper.

"I write poetry, Mrs. Hicks," he said.

"Well, I shouldn't think that's very difficult, is it?" said Mrs. Hicks. "I'd write it meself if I had time."

This was rather damping. Ern tried again. "I'd like to know what you think of my last pome," he said. "Can I say it to you?"

"If you like," said Mrs. Hicks, still rolling the pastry vigorously. "Silly stuff really. I used to do reciting at school meself."

"But this is something I made up," said Ern. "At least – I made up some of it, and a friend of mine made up the other half." And with that he stood up and recited his verses – and Fatty's – about the "Poor Old House". He didn't see Mr. Goon at the kitchen door, standing amazed at Ern's recital. He almost jumped out of his skin when he heard his uncle's voice at the end.

"Have you taken to poetry writing again, Ern?" said Mr. Goon. "How many times have I told you it's a waste of time? Do you remember that rude poem you wrote about me, once? Well, *I* haven't forgotten it, see? And what's all that about 'The Ivies' in that poem? Don't you go putting secret information like that into your poems. You give me that notebook of yours and let me see what other poems you've got there."

"No, Uncle. My notebook's private," said Ern, remembering that he had put into it notes of the meetings he had had with Fatty and the others.

"Now, look here, young Ern," said Goon, advancing on him, and Ern promptly fled out of the back-door. He saw a black shadow moving before him, and yelled.

61

"Uncle! There's someone out here! Quick, uncle!"

Mr. Goon rushed out at once – and ran straight into Mrs. Hicks' washing-line, which was hung with overalls, two sheets and a dark blanket. The line broke, and Mr. Goon gave a yell as the blanket folded itself round him.

Poor Ern! He really had thought that the washing blowing in the darkness on the line was somebody in the yard. When he saw his uncle staggering into the kitchen with the washing dragging behind him on the broken line, he knew there was only one thing to do – and that was to rush up to his bedroom and lock himself in!

That means going without his supper – but at least he still had his precious notebook and at least he was safe from his uncle's anger. Judging from the noise downstairs he was lucky to have escaped in time. Why, oh why had he ever said he would come and help his uncle? Never again, thought poor Ern. Never again!

Meantime Fatty was feeling that he had come to a full stop where the mysterious notes were concerned. They hadn't found a house called The Ivies, or even one with ivy growing up it that *had* been called The Ivies. Neither had they found the right Smith. Was there anything else to do?

"Only one thing," thought Fatty. "And that will be a terribly fiddling job. I'd better try and get the letters and words off, that are stuck on to the sheet of writing-paper. I might find something printed on the other side to help me – I might even find out what newspaper they come from. If it was, say, a Bristol paper, the odds are that the writer of the notes comes from Bristol – or if it turns out to by a Manchester paper, maybe he comes from Manchester. Not that that will be much help."

So he went down to his shed that evening and set to work. It was indeed a horribly fiddling job. In the middle of it, his lamp flickered and went out.

"Blow!" said Fatty, and gathered up his things by the light of a candle and went indoors. He sat himself down in his bedroom to finish the job.

He found a few interesting things as he tried to get the pasted-on letters off the strips they were stuck on. The word "goon" for instance, which was, in every case, apparently part of a whole word – it was not made of four separate letters. Fatty stared at it. "Goon". It must be part of a whole word. But what word had "goon" in it. He couldn't think of any.

As he went on with his work, a tap came at the door, and his mother came in. "Frederick, have you taken my library book?" she asked. "Good gracious, whatever are you doing? What a mess!"

"I'm just solving a – well, a kind of puzzle really," said Fatty. His mother picked up the cut-out piece of paper he had just put down – the bit with "goon" on.

"Goon," she said. "What a funny puzzle, Frederick. Is that part of 'Rangoon' or something?"

"*Ran*goon!" said Fatty. "I never thought of Rangoon. It's about the only word ending in 'goon', isn't it, Mother? Has Rangoon been in the papers much lately? Has anything happened there? Would the name be printed a lot in our papers?"

"Well no – I can't remember seeing anything about Rangoon," said his mother. "Oh Frederick – you *have* got my library book! Really, that's too bad of you."

"Gosh, sorry, Mother – I must have brought it up by mistake," said Fatty. "It's almost exactly like mine, look."

"Would you like me to stay and help you to sort out this queer puzzle?" asked his mother. "I like puzzles, as you know."

"Oh no, Mother, thank you, I wouldn't dream of bothering you," said Fatty, hastily, afraid of some awkward questions as to where he had got the "puzzle" from. "It's hopeless, really. I expect I'll have to give it up."

And that is exactly what poor Fatty had to do, after struggling with it for at least two hours. There was nothing on the other side of the pasted-on letters that could help him to identify any newspapers – only odd letters

63

that might have come from any part of any paper. It was very disappointing.

"*That* idea's no good then," said Fatty, putting the bits and pieces back into the envelope. "Waste of two hours! I'm at a dead-end. Can't find any clues at all – and even when there was a chance of actually *seeing* that fellow who delivers the notes, Ern doesn't see him. He must have had forty winks – he couldn't have failed to see him if he was really awake. Blow! Where do we go from here? I'll call a meeting tomorrow morning, and we'll see if anyone has any ideas."

So next morning, at ten o'clock sharp, everyone was at Fatty's, including Ern. Ern was feeling a bit happier. His uncle had had a nice letter from Superintendent Jenks that morning, about some small case that Goon had apparently handled quite well – and the big police-man had beamed all through breakfast. He read the letter to Ern three times, very solemnly.

"Now if *I* had done what *you* did yesterday, and sat looking out of that window of yours, keeping watch, and hadn't even *seen* something going on under my very nose, I wouldn't be getting letters like this," said Goon.

Ern didn't argue. He nodded his head and helped him-self to more bread and butter and marmalade. He made up his mind to go up to Fatty's immediately after break-fast and tell him he was going home. He was sure that his uncle wouldn't pay him any more wages, and he wasn't going to stop with him for nothing!

So Ern was at the meeting too. When they were all in the shed, Fatty told them of his failure the night before. "Mother came up and offered to help me," he said. "But I was afraid she'd ask me awkward questions. She did say that she thought the word 'goon' with the small letter instead of the capital one, might be part of *Ran*goon. And it *might*, though I can't think how it could help us! I gave up trying to find a clue by unpasting the letters in the messages. And now I don't really see what else we can do."

"Well, there's only *one* thing left," said Daisy, "and that's that place that Larry and I found. What was it called now – Fairlin Hall. The place that was empty. I just wondered if it might be worth while finding out if it had *ever* been called 'The Ivies'."

"But you said it was empty," said Fatty. "You saw a notice-board up, saying that it was for sale."

"Yes, I know," said Daisy. "But I went by it today – just out of curiosity, you know – and I saw something queer."

"What?" asked everyone at once.

"Well – I'm sure there was smoke coming out of a chimney at the back," said Daisy. "I couldn't be *quite* certain – the chimney might have belonged to a house I couldn't see. But it did *look* as if a chimney belonging to Fairlin Hall itself was smoking."

"Well! This certainly needs investigating," said Fatty, cheering up at once. "There might be someone hiding there – Smith perhaps! I vote we all cycle down straightaway and have a snoop round. What about it, everyone? Come on!"

And out they all rushed to get their bicycles, with Buster barking madly round them. Was this a clue to the mystery – or wasn't it? A smoking chimney! If only it *did* belong to Fairlin Hall!

The Caretakers at Fairlin Hall

The six cyclists, with Buster panting behind, rode through Peterswood at top speed. It was most unfortunate that they should meet Mr. Goon round a corner. He was on his bicycle too, and Ern, being on the middle of the road, almost ran into him.

"Ern!" yelled Mr. Goon, wobbling dangerously. "I'll

65

teach you to – here, where are you going, Ern! ERN!"

But Ern, and the others too, were away up the road, Ern looking scared. "Hope he won't come after me," he said. He looked round, and to his horror saw that Mr. Goon had swung round and was pedalling furiously some way behind them.

"Can't let him see us going into Fairlin Hall," panted Fatty. "We'll go right past it, and up Cockers Hill. Goon will soon be left behind then."

So they swept past Fairlin Hall, each trying to see whether smoke was coming from any chimney, turned the corner and made for the steep Cockers Hill. Up they went, more slowly now, hearing Mr. Goon's shouts for Ern faintly behind them. Bets began to giggle.

"Oh dear! Mr. Goon will be as red as a beetroot when he's half-way up this hill! It's rather a shame, Fatty."

"He doesn't *need* to follow us up it," panted Fatty, who was a good deal too plump for such violent exercise. "Look behind, Bets. Has he dismounted yet?"

Bets glanced behind. "Yes, he has. He's standing still, mopping his head. Poor Goon! We'll soon shake him off."

They came to the top of Cockers Hill, sailed down it thankfully, and then made their way back to the road in which Fairlin Hall stood. There was no sign of Goon anywhere. They put their bicycles against the wall, and stood at the gate entrance, looking into the drive.

"See what I mean," said Daisy, eagerly. "Isn't that smoke from one of the chimneys right at the back of the house?"

"Yes. I rather think it is," said Fatty. "What an ugly old place! Look at those great pillars at the front door – and those heavy stone balconies. It must have been empty for years."

He went to look at the "For Sale" board, and noted the House Agent's name on it. "Paul and Ticking," he said. "It wouldn't be a bad idea to go and ask them for particulars of this place – we might find out if it had ever been called 'The Ivies'."

"Yes. That's a good idea!" said Pip. "Well – shall we snoop round the place and see if anyone's about? We must find out if that smoking chimney belongs to the house."

"Yes," said Fatty. "I'll go with Bets. You stay here, you three, out of sight, with Buster. Bets and I will go round to the back of the house, calling Buster, as if we'd lost him, and if anyone *is* there, they'll probably come out to us. When we've stopped yelling for Buster, you can let him go, and he'll come to us."

"Right," said Larry, catching hold of the little Scottie by the collar. Fatty and Bets made their way down the overgrown drive, Fatty calling "Buster, Buster, where are you?" at the top of his voice. Buster nearly went mad trying to follow, and was extremely angry with Larry for hanging on to his collar. He almost choked himself, trying to get away.

Fatty peeped into the windows he passed. The house was as dismal inside as it was outside. Great empty rooms, dirty and dreary, with filthy windows, and faded paint – Bets shivered, and turned her face away.

They rounded a corner and came to the kitchen end. There was a line across the yard, with clothes blowing on it – aha, there was certainly someone here, then! Fatty nudged Bets and glanced upwards. Bets did the same and saw a chimney above, smoking. Daisy had been right.

"Buster, Buster, where are you, you naughty dog!" shouted Fatty, and whistled piercingly.

An oldish woman came out of the kitchen door, thin and sad-looking, but with a kindly, rather sweet old face. "Have you lost your dog?" she said.

"He's somewhere about," said Fatty truthfully. "I do hope I didn't disturb you. Isn't this place empty? I saw a 'For Sale' notice outside."

"That's right," said the woman, pulling her shawl round her. "We're caretakers. The house was left quite

67

empty for years, but tramps kept breaking in – so the agents put in caretakers. We've been here for fifteen years now – and we hope the place *won't* be sold, because we don't want to be turned out!"

Buster suddenly came rushing round the corner, and barked madly when he saw Fatty. He was most indignant at being held so long by Larry, who, of course, had let him go as soon as Fatty had stopped calling him.

"Ah – there's your dog," said the old woman. "He couldn't have been far away. I sometimes wish *we* had a dog. Three times since we've been here there's been burglars – though what they expect to find in an empty house, I *don't* know!"

A voice called her from indoors, and then someone coughed long and painfully. "That's my poor husband," said the old woman. "He's ill. I suppose you aren't going back to the village, are you? I ought to go to the chemist and get him some more medicine, but I don't really like leaving him."

"Of course we'll leave a message at the chemist for you – or better still we'll pop down and get the medicine ourselves and bring it back!" said Fatty. "We've got our bicycles."

"Well, that would be real kind of you," said the old lady. "I'll just get the bottle," and she hurried indoors.

"Wonder if their name is Smith," said Fatty, in a low voice. "Shouldn't think so. Obviously they're just caretakers who've been here for years. Ah – here she comes."

"Here's the bottle," said the old woman. "And here's the shilling for the medicine. Ask for the same prescription as before, please."

"Er – what name shall I say?" asked Fatty.

"Smith," said the old lady. "Mr. John Smith. The chemist will know."

"Right," said Fatty, startled to hear that there *was* a Mr. Smith in this ivy-covered place. He glanced at Bets, and saw that she was astonished too. "Come on, Buster, old thing. We'll be back in about ten minutes, Mrs. Smith."

"You're kind, real kind," she said, and gave them a smile that made her old face quite beautiful.

Fatty and Bets ran back up the drive with Buster at their heels. Fatty's thoughts were in a whirl. Was this another wrong Smith – or could it be – could it *possibly* be the right one?

"What an awfully long time you were," said Larry. "What happened?"

Fatty told the others briefly, as they wheeled their bicycles into the road. "Two caretakers there – been in charge of the house for fifteen years. And the name is SMITH! What do you think of that?"

"Come on – we're going to the chemist," said Bets.

"What on earth for?" demanded Pip.

"Tell you as we go," said Fatty, which was really rather a dangerous thing to do, as the other four were so keen to hear Fatty's tale that they rode in a close bunch as near to him as possible, their pedals almost touching! However, they arrived at the chemist's safely, and Fatty went in with the bottle, planning to get a little more information about the Smiths if he could.

"For Mr. Smith?" said the chemist, who knew Fatty. "How's the old fellow? He's been ailing for the past year. He really ought to get out of that damp old place, and go and live by the sea – but they're as poor as church mice."

"Mrs. Smith seemed very nice," said Fatty. "I don't know her husband."

"He's a queer fellow," said the chemist, writing out a label. "Sort of scared. Hardly ever goes out, and when his wife was ill, and he had to come in to get medicine for her, he hardly opened his mouth. I guess they don't want that old place to be sold – they'd have to look for somewhere else to go to, and that's not easy these days, when you're old and poor."

"Who used to own Fairlin Hall?" asked Fatty.

"I've no idea," said the chemist. "It's been empty for years – long before *I* came here. Falling to pieces, I should think. It's a dismal place. Well, there you are. One shilling, please, and give my kind regards to the old lady. She's a pet, and simply worships the old man."

"Thanks," said Fatty, and went out with Bets. "We'll go straight back to Fairlin Hall," he said to the others, who were waiting outside. "I'll see if I can get any more information out of Mrs. Smith. Then we'll go the House Agent. We simply MUST find out if that house was ever called The Ivies – if it was, we're really on the track of the mystery!"

They all went back to Fairlin Hall, and Fatty and Bets once more went round to the back door, this time with Buster free, dancing round them. The kitchen door was shut, and they knocked.

"If that's the medicine, would you leave it on the door-step?" called the old woman's voice. "I'm just seeing to my husband. He's had a nasty coughing attack. Thank you very very much."

Fatty put the bottle down on the step, rather disappointed at not being able to get any more information. He took a quick look round. The yard was very clean and tidy. Spotless, well-mended curtains hung at the windows – the only clean windows in the house! The doorstep was well-scrubbed. A washed milk-bottle stood there, waiting for the milkman.

"Well – Mr. Smith *may* be a man with a false name and a queer past of some sort," said Fatty, as they went back to the others. "But there's nothing wrong with the old lady. Even the chemist said she was a pet. I liked her, didn't you, Bets?"

"Yes, I did," said Bets. "Oh dear – I do hope nothing horrid will happen to Mr. Smith, it would make his wife so unhappy. The man who wrote those notes didn't seem to like him at all, did he? I wonder what he meant by telling Mr. Goon to say SECRETS to him."

"Can't imagine," said Fatty. "Well now – off we go to

the House Agent's. Hallo – what's all the noise going on outside the front gates?"

Fatty soon found out! Mr. Goon had come cycling by and had suddenly seen Larry, Daisy, Pip – and Ern! He also saw Fatty's bicycle and Bets', leaning against the wall, and felt very curious indeed. He had dismounted heavily from his own bicycle, after making sure that Buster was nowhere around, and demanded to know what they were all doing there.

"Just having a bit of a rest," said Pip. "Going up Cockers Hill at top speed was tiring, Mr. Goon. I expect you found it so, too."

"I don't want any cheek," said Mr. Goon, glaring at Pip. "Where's that fat boy gone? What's he here for? Ho – another ivy-covered house! Snooping round again, I suppose. Well, you won't find much there – it's empty, see? Ern – you come here."

Just at that moment Fatty and Bets and Buster came out of the gate, and Buster ran barking in delight towards his old enemy. Goon leapt on his bicycle at once, and rode off quickly, shouting to Ern.

"You come back with me, young Ern. I've got a job for you, delivering messages. You come at once, Ern."

"Better go, Ern," said Fatty. "Who knows – he may give you some more wages at dinner-time, if you do some work for him this morning!"

"What a hope!" said Ern, in disgust. "All right, Fatty. I'll go, if you say so. I'll be down at your place as soon as I can to hear your news. So long!"

And away he went after his uncle, looking so doleful that the others couldn't help laughing. "Now to the House Agent's," said Fatty, mounting his bicycle too. "I feel we're getting somewhere now!"

Mr. Grimble talks

The House Agent's office was in the middle of the High Street, and its window was set out with all kinds of very dull particulars of houses for sale.

"I hope you won't be too long, Fatty," said Pip. "It's a bit boring for the rest of us, waiting about while you and Bets do the work."

"Sorry!" said Fatty. "Yes, you're right – I've been making you wait about half the morning. Look, go into the dairy, and order what you like. It's gone eleven o'clock, I should think. I'll pay. I've still got heaps left from my Christmas money. Bets, you go too, and order me two macaroons and an ice-cream."

"Oh *Fatty* – didn't you have any breakfast!" said Bets. But Fatty had already disappeared into the House Agent's office. A young man was there, very busy at a big desk. In a corner, at a much smaller desk, sat a clerk, an older man, round-shouldered and shabby.

"Well – what can I do for *you*?" said the young man.

"Have you any particulars about Fairlin Hall?" asked Fatty, politely. The young man stared at him.

"That old place! You're not thinking of buying it, by any chance, are you?" he said, and laughed.

"Well, no," said Fatty. "I'm – er – interested in its history, to tell you the truth."

"Well, I'm sorry – but I haven't time to give you a history lesson," said the young man rudely. "The place has been empty as long as I can remember – since before I was born. We're hoping to sell it as a school of some sort, but it's in such bad condition, nobody will buy. It's got no history as far as *I* know!"

The telephone bell rang at that moment, and the young man picked up the receiver. "Mr. Paul here," he said. "Oh *yes*, Mrs. Donning. Yes, yes, yes. Of course, of course. No trouble at all. Do give me all the particulars."

It was quite plain to Fatty that he wasn't going to get any help from the bumptious Mr. Paul, who was evidently one of the partners in the business of Paul and Ticking. He turned and made for the door.

But as he passed the old clerk in the corner, he heard a few quiet words. "I can tell you something about the house if you like, sir."

Fatty turned and saw that the old man was trying to make up for Mr. Paul's rudeness. He went over to his desk.

"Do you know anything about the place?" he said, eagerly. "You know it, don't you – covered with ivy from top to bottom."

"Oh yes. I sold it to its present owners twenty-one years ago," said the clerk. "It was a lovely place then. I and my wife used to know the old lady who lived there. Ah, Fairlin Hall was well-kept then – it had four gardeners, and you should have seen the rose-garden! I was talking about it to old Grimble only the other day. He was head gardener there, and knew every corner of it."

Fatty pricked up his ears at once. Surely an old gardener would know far more about Fairlin Hall than anyone else He might be pleased to talk about the old place, too.

"Perhaps you could give me Grimble's address," he said. "Does he still work?"

"Oh no – he's retired. Just potters about his own garden," said the old clerk. "I'll scribble down his address for you."

"Er – was Fairlin Hall ever called anything else?" asked Fatty, hopefully.

"I believe it was – but I can't remember," said the old man. "But perhaps I can look it up for you."

"Potter!" said Mr. Paul, putting down the telephone receiver, "it's very difficult for me to telephone, with you jabbering in the corner."

"Sorry, Mr. Paul," said poor old Potter, and hastily pushed a piece of paper over to Fatty, who shot out of the office before the rude Mr. Paul could admonish him too. Ugh! Fancy that old clerk having to put up with young Mr. Paul's rudeness all the time! Fatty glanced down at the piece of paper he had been given.

"Donald Grimble," he read. "Primrose Cot, Burling Meadows. Gardener."

He ran across the road to the dairy, where all the others were now sitting round a table, eating macaroons. Buster greeted him loudly as usual, barking as if he hadn't seen Fatty for at least a month.

"You haven't been long, Fatty," said Bets. "I've only taken two bites at my macaroon. Have one – they're lovely and fresh. All gooey."

"Did you find out anything?" asked Larry.

Fatty told them about the rude Mr. Paul and the nice old man in the corner who seemed so scared of him. Then he showed them the piece of paper. "Donald Grimble used to be head gardener at Fairlin Hall," he said, "and apparently knew every corner of the place. He's retired now – but I bet he can tell us plenty about it. If ONLY we could find out if it has ever been called 'The Ivies'! I can't help thinking that old Mr. Smith, whose medicine we got this morning, *must* be the Smith referred to in those anonymous notes."

"We've got time to go and see Grimble this morning," said Bets. "But what excuse can we make? He'll wonder why we're so interested in the old place. He might think we were making fun of him, or something."

"I know! Let's buy a pot with some queer plant in at the florist's," said Daisy, "and go and ask him to tell us what it is! Then we can get talking."

"Daisy, that's a very bright idea," said Fatty, approvingly, and Daisy went red with pleasure. "That will mean we can all go, instead of most of you waiting about outside. I'll have another macaroon, please."

"I suppose you're counting, Fatty?" said Pip, handing

him the plate. "You've had three already, and they're expensive, you know. Even *your* Christmas money won't last long if you empty plates of macaroons at this rate.'

"Have an ice-cream, Pip," said Fatty, "and stop counting how many macaroons I eat. Bets, aren't *you* going to have an ice-cream? You'd better feed yourself up, because I'm going to make *you* take the pot-plant in to old Mr. Grimble!"

"Oh *no*!" said Bets. "Why can't one of the others?"

"Because you have a very nice smile, Bets, enough to melt the crabbed old heart of even a fierce head gardener!" said Fatty.

Bets laughed. "You might be Irish, Fatty, with all your blarney!" she said. "All right, I'll do it for you. Shall Daisy and I go and buy the plant now, while you others are finishing? We can't eat another thing."

"Yes. Here's the money," said Fatty, but Daisy pushed it away. "Oddly enough, *I* have some Christmas money left too!" she said. "Come on, Bets – let's leave these guzzlers, and go to the flower shop."

They were back again with a small plant just as the three boys and Buster came out of the dairy, looking rather well-fed.

"Please, Mr. Grimble," said Bets, looking up at Fatty with a smile, "could you tell me what this plant is?"

Fatty laughed. "Fine, Bets! But be sure to get *us* into the picture somehow, so that we can come and listen – and so that I can ask questions!"

They went off to Burling Meadows on their bicycles. Primrose Cot was a small cottage standing by itself in a beautiful little garden. Not a weed showed in the smooth grass lawn. Nor was there a weed in any of the beds, either. The hedges were trim and neat. Early snowdrops showed their little white bonnets under a tree, and yellow aconites wore their pretty green frills just beside them.

"That must be old Grimble sawing logs at the bottom of the garden," said Fatty, seeing a sturdy old man there, a battered hat at the back of his head, and the dark blue apron of a head gardener over his corduroy trousers. "Let's go into the field nearby and speak to him over the hedge."

So they went down a side-path into the field that skirted the bottom of Grimble's garden. Bets called to him over the hedge. "Please, are you Mr. Grimble?"

"Yes, I am," answered the old fellow, peering over at Bets. "What do you want with me?"

"Oh please, could you tell me what this plant is?" asked Bets, with her sweetest smile, and handed up the pot. "It's got such pretty leaves, and I do want to know its name. You know the names of every plant, don't you, Mr. Grimble?"

Grimble beamed down at her. "Well, I know a tidy few, Missie. This here plant is a young Coleus – but you want to take it home and keep it in the warm. It don't like cold air."

"Have you ever grown Coleuses?" asked Bets.

"Oh aye! Thousands," said old Grimble. "I used to work at that old place, Fairlin Hall – I were head gardener there for years – and I always kept one corner of the heated greenhouse for them Coleus. Pretty things they are, with their patterned leaves – all colours!"

"Oh, Fatty – he used to work at Fairlin Hall," called Bets, anxious to bring the others into the conversation. "Wasn't that the place we saw this morning – you know, where that old woman lives, whose husband we fetched medicine for."

Fatty came up at once, pleased with Bets. The others followed, amused at her little performance.

"Good morning," said Fatty, politely. "Yes, we did go into the front drive and round to the back this morning. We didn't see much of the garden though."

"Ah, it's a terrible place now," said Grimble, sadly. "I worked there, man and boy, for years, young sir, and was made head gardener. You should have seen my roses – 'twas a show-place, my rose garden. I never go down that road now – can't abear to see my old garden gone to ruin."

"The house is absolutely *covered* with ivy now," said Pip, putting in a word himself. "Even the chimneys are green with it. Was it covered with ivy when you were there, Mr. Grimble?"

"Oh yes – but not as thick as it is now," said Grimble. "My father planted that ivy, so he told me. It weren't called Fairlin Hall then, you know. It were called The Ivies."

This welcome bit of news came so suddenly that all the children had quite a shock. So they were right! Fairlin Hall *was* once The Ivies! It *was* the house spoken of in those anonymous notes. But how strange that the writer didn't know that it had a different name now – it had been called Fairlin Hall for years and years!

"Why was the name changed?" asked Fatty.

Grimble looked at him and said nothing for some twenty seconds. Then he spoke in a curiously sad voice. "The Ivies got a bad name," he said. "Something happened there. My master and mistress, Colonel and Mrs. Hasterley, couldn't abear their home to be pointed at – it were in all the papers, you see – and they sold up and went. And when new people bought the place, they changed the name. Yes – it were once The Ivies – but that's a long time since."

The children were silent for a minute or two, and the old gardener began his sawing again, looking sad and far-away.

"What happened?" ventured Fatty, at last. "Was it – was it something bad that your master did?"

"Nay – he were as good a man as ever lived," said old Grimble. "It were his son, Master Wilfrid, that brought shame on the old place, and on his parents too." And to the children's horror, tears gathered in the old man's eyes, and dripped onto his saw!

"Let's go," said Fatty, at once. "Come on – let's go."

Mr. Goon is pleased with himself

The five murmured a quiet good-bye to old Grimble, who took no notice at all. He was evidently lost in far-off memories, which were still powerful enough to upset him. They all felt very sorry to have made the old fellow weep. Bets felt tears in her own eyes.

"We shouldn't have asked him questions, Fatty," she said. "I feel dreadful about it."

"Well, we couldn't tell that he would take it like that," said Fatty, feeling rather uncomfortable himself. "My word, though – we were right. Fairlin Hall *was* The Ivies. I wonder what dreadful thing Wilfrid Hasterley did to bring the house such shame and notoriety – enough to make its name known all over the country, and force his parents to sell it."

"We'd better find out," said Larry. "How can we?"

"I almost think I'd better ask Superintendent Jenks about it," said Fatty. "If he can tell us what the shocking happening was, it might make all this business of the anonymous notes a bit clearer. It's plain that the writer wants old Smith to be cleared out of Fairlin Hall – and it's also plain that he, the writer, must have been away for a good long time, if he doesn't know that the name has been changed for twenty years or more. It's a proper mystery, this!"

"You'd better telephone the Super when you get home, Fatty," said Larry. "Gosh, it's almost one o'clock! Daisy, come on – we'll be late for lunch!"

Fatty went home thinking hard. There were a great many questions in this mystery that had no answers. Who was the writer of the notes? How did he keep putting them where Goon could find them, and yet never be

78

seen himself? Why didn't he know that The Ivies was now Fairlin Hall, and had been for years? Why did he want Smith sent out of Fairlin Hall – and why did Smith apparently have a false name?

"Too *many* mysteries this time," said Fatty, cycling home fast. "Well – the time has come to tackle the Super about it. I'll telephone immediately after my lunch."

He went to the telephone at two o'clock, hoping that The Super might have finished his own lunch. Alas, he was away in the north of England. His deputy, who knew a little about Fatty's amateur detective work, was sympathetic, but not very helpful.

"You could go and see Mr. Goon, the constable in your village," he suggested. "He might be able to help you. In fact, Master Frederick, I think that is the thing you *should* do. I believe we have had information from Mr. Goon that some rather peculiar anonymous notes have been arriving at his house, and if you know anything that ties up with those, it's your duty to inform him. I'll tell the Super when he comes back – but I don't expect him for some days."

This was extremely disappointing. Fatty put down the telephone with a groan. Blow! Now he'd *have* to go to Goon! The Super would not be at all pleased with him if he held up his information just because he wasn't friendly with Goon. He sat down and considered the matter.

"Well – it's no good. I'd better get it over," thought Fatty. "I'll cycle down to Goon's house now. How cocka-hoop he'll be to think I'm passing on my information to him. Well – I jolly well shan't tell him HOW I got it!"

Fatty fetched his bicycle and went off to Goon's, feeling decidedly down in the dumps. He knew quite well that Goon would pretend to the Super that *he* had found out most of the information himself, and give no credit to Fatty and the others. He came to Goon's house and knocked at the door. Mrs. Hicks opened it, breathless and panting, as if she had been running a mile.

"Mr. Goon's not in," she told him. "But Ern is. Do you want to see him? He's up in his room, watching out of the window. We had another of them ominous notes this morning."

Fatty was interested. He went up to Ern's room, and found the boy sitting close to his window, his eyes glued on the yard below. "I heard your voice, Fatty," he said, without turning round. "I'm on the watch again. We've had another note this morning – pegged to the washing line it was!"

"What – right in the middle of the yard!" said Fatty, astonished. "I must say the writer's bold. Nobody saw him, I suppose?"

"No," said Ern. "But nobody was watching. Funny note it was. It didn't say 'The Ivies' this time. It said Fairlin Hall. 'Ask Smith at Fairlin Hall what his real name is,' that's what it said."

"Oho! So the writer has at last found out that The Ivies has changed its name," said Fatty. "I suppose this means that your uncle has gone racing round to Fairlin Hall, Ern?"

"Yes," said Ern. "He wasn't half pleased about it, either – getting in on Mr. Smith like that. He doesn't know that you saw old Mrs. Smith this morning, and found out so much."

"Poor old Smith," said Fatty. "I wouldn't like to be in *his* shoes when old Goon asks him questions. He'll be pretty beastly to the poor fellow. I think I'll stay here till he comes back, Ern. He may have some news. Gosh – to think we've all been working so hard to find out if Fairlin Hall was once The Ivies – and now Goon's been lucky enough to have the information handed to him in one of those notes!"

A scream came suddenly from downstairs, and made Fatty and Ern jump. "That's Mrs. Hicks," said Ern, and they both ran downstairs. Mrs. Hicks was lying back in the kitchen arm-chair, fanning herself with the dish-cloth.

"What's the matter?" cried Ern.

"Another note!" wailed Mrs. Hicks. "I went to my larder just now – and there was a note, pushed in through the larder window – on top of the fish, it was. It give me such a turn, seeing it there. You go and get it, Ern. I'm getting so as I don't want to touch the things. Horrible ominous notes!"

Fatty went to the larder before Ern. He looked in at the open door, and saw the square envelope lying on top of a plate of fish, just beside the open larder window. He took it and tore it open, though he knew he ought to wait for Mr. Goon.

"Found out about Smith yet, you dunder-head?" said the note, in the familiar cut-out, pasted letters.

"When did you go to the larder last, Mrs. Hicks?" demanded Fatty.

"About twenty minutes ago," said Mrs. Hicks. "The note wasn't there then, I'll swear it wasn't. I got some fish for the cat, off that dish – and put it back again on the shelf."

"It *couldn't* have been put there in the last twenty minutes," said Ern, at once. "Haven't I been watching out of that window for the last half-hour? You know I have!"

"Ah, but your friend went up to see you," said Mrs. Hicks. "The note must have come then, when you were talking to him and not keeping a watch."

"I *was* watching," said Ern, angrily. "I never took my eyes off the yard. Did I, Fatty?"

"Well, *I* heard you talking all right," said Mrs. Hicks. "And when people talk, they can't watch too. *You'll* catch it from that uncle of yours!"

"I don't know how the messenger has the nerve to walk across the yard and back like that," said Fatty. "He must know that Ern was watching – he could easily see him at the bedroom window. It must mean that the messenger hides himself somewhere very near, and watches his chance."

"That's it, sir," said Mrs. Hicks. "Artful as a bagful of

81

monkeys he is. I've never seen him – though once or twice I've thought I heard him. It scares me proper, it does."

"There's Uncle," said Ern, looking suddenly anxious. "Loveaduck – won't he be angry with me when he hears there's another note, left under our noses – me watching and all!"

Mr. Goon came in, whistling softly. "Pleased with himself!" said Ern, looking at Fatty. Goon walked into the kitchen, calling to Mrs. Hicks.

"A cup of tea, please, Mrs. Hicks. Hallo – you here, Master Frederick? And why aren't you watching at your window, Ern?"

"Er – well, Mrs. Hicks found another note, Uncle," said Ern, warily. "And she screamed, and me and Fatty, we shot down to see what was the matter."

"Well – there won't be any *more* notes," said Goon. "Not as soon as the writer of them hears that old Smith has gone from Fairlin Hall. I sent him packing!"

"But why, Mr. Goon?" asked Fatty, troubled to think that poor old Mrs. Smith should have had to turn out with her sick husband.

"Come into the office," said Goon, who was looking very pleased with himself. "Do you good, Master Frederick, to hear how the police can get to work and settle things." Fatty and Ern followed him, leaving Mrs. Hicks alone in the kitchen, looking annoyed at being left out.

"Sit down," ordered Goon, and Ern and Fatty obediently sat down. Goon leaned back and put his finger-tips together, looking at the two boys in a most irritating way.

"Well, acting on information received, I went round to Fairlin Hall – you probably don't know, but it was once called The Ivies," began Goon. "And there I found this fellow Smith, talked about in those notes. His wife was most obstructive – said he was ill, and I wasn't to disturb him – such nerve to tell *me* that," frowned Goon.

"Well, I soon told her I wasn't standing any nonsense, and pushed her aside ..."

"Not really *pushed*!" said Fatty, horrified to think of the gentle old lady being roughly handled by the big policeman.

"Well, shoved, if you want a better word," grinned Goon. "And there was Smith, in bed – *pretending* to be ill, of course. Well, I made him get out – couldn't let him get away with a lot of humbug like that – and I said to him, 'Now then! What are you masquerading round under a false name for? You tell me *that*!'"

There was a pause, presumably for Ern and Fatty to exclaim in admiration of Goon's behaviour with the Smiths. As neither of them said a word, he went on, not at all taken aback.

"Well, the old woman got hold of my arm, and began to sob – all put on, of course. She said their name wasn't Smith, it was Canley – and that rang a bell with me, that did! *Canley!* He was a bad lot, he was – he sold the secrets of a new war-plane of ours to the enemy, and he went to jail for years. Ha – and when he came out, he had to report to the police every so often, but he didn't – he just took a false name and disappeared! Helped by that wife of his, of course. She waited for him all the time he was in jail."

"So that was what the word 'SECRETS' meant, in that note," said Fatty, quite disgusted with Goon's hard-hearted narrative. "Smith – or Canley – would react to that word at once, be afraid – and pack up and go."

"That's right," said Goon. "And that's just what I told him to do – pack up and go! Can't have a man like that in a responsible position as caretaker."

"But he was ill," said Fatty, "and his wife is old. Poor things."

"Ill! No, he was putting that on," snorted Goon. "He might deceive you, but he couldn't deceive *me*. I told him he's got to report to me here tomorrow morning, then we'll go into all this. Then I left. Now we know what all those notes meant!"

"We don't," said Fatty, shaking his head. "All we know is that someone had a spite against old Smith and wanted him out of Fairlin Hall. We don't know what the real reason was. There must be *some* reason!"

"You'll wear your brains out, you will," said Goon. "There's no mystery left, so don't pretend there is. Think yourself lucky that I've told you the end of it – fiddling about with Ivies and Smiths and Secrets. It's all plain as the nose on your face. I've settled it!"

He turned to Ern. "You can go home, Ern. There's no more watching to do. I don't know who sent those notes and I don't care. He put me on to a man the police want to keep their eyes on – and the Super will be pleased about *that*! I'll get another Letter of Commendation, you see if I don't!"

"Well, you wouldn't get one from *me*," said Fatty, standing up. "You'd no right to treat a poor old woman and an ill man so roughly. And let me tell you this – you think you've washed out this mystery – but you haven't! You'll never wear *your* brains out, Mr. Goon – you don't use them enough!"

Fatty is a great help

Fatty stalked out of Goon's office, paying no attention to his snorts of anger. "Go and get your things, Ern," he said. "You needn't go home just yet. You can come with me. Whatever Goon says, this mystery isn't settled. There's a lot more to it than hounding old Smith out of Fairlin Hall!"

"Coo, Fatty! Can I really come with you?" said Ern, overjoyed. He shot upstairs, and was soon down again with his small bag. He didn't even say good-bye to his uncle.

"We'll call a meeting at once," said Fatty. "I'll telephone to ... no ... I don't think I will. There's something else more urgent. Ern, the Smiths may still be at Fairlin Hall, packing up to go – arranging for their bits and pieces of furniture to be moved. Let's go down there and see."

"Right. Anything you say," said Ern, giving Fatty a worshipping look. Loveaduck! Fatty was worth ten Mr. Goons any day, the way he always knew what to do!

In a few minutes they had cycled to Fairlin Hall, and went round the back to the kitchen quarters. As Fatty had thought, the Smiths were still there. But they were not packing!

Mr. Smith was lying on the floor, and the old lady was kneeling beside him, weeping, and wiping his forehead with a damp cloth. "John!" she was saying. "John, I'm here. I'm going to get the doctor, dearie. Open your eyes! I'm going to get the doctor."

She didn't even hear the two boys open the door and come in. Fatty had looked through the window, and had seen what was happening. She jumped violently when he touched her gently on the arm.

"Mrs. Smith," he said. "I'll get the doctor for you. Let Ern and I lift your husband back into bed. He seems very ill."

"Oh, he is, he is," wept the old lady, recognizing Fatty as the boy who had gone to the chemist for her. "He's just had a terrible shock too – I can't tell you what it was – and we've been told to go. But where *can* we go, young sir – and him as ill as that?"

"Now listen," said Fatty, gently. "Let us get your husband back into bed. We'll get the doctor – and probably an ambulance, because I'm sure your husband ought to be in hospital. That's the first thing to do."

He and Ern managed to get the old man back into bed. He murmured something and half-opened his eyes, then began to cough in a terrible manner. His old wife wiped his face with the damp cloth, and comforted him. Ern's eyes filled with tears, and he looked desperately at Fatty.

"Don't worry, Ern," said Fatty. "We'll soon put this right. Stay here and do what you can to help Mrs. Smith. I'm going to telephone the doctor. Who is your doctor, Mrs. Smith?"

She told him, and Fatty nodded. "He's mine too – so that's fine. I'll be back soon."

Fatty ran to the nearest kiosk to telephone, and Dr. Rainy listened in surprise to what he had to say.

"Well, well – the poor old fellow! I saw him yesterday and told Mrs. Smith I'd send an ambulance to take him to hospital, but she wouldn't hear of it. I'll get one along at once and arrange for a bed for him in the Cottage Hospital here. See you later!"

Fatty raced back to Fairlin Hall. The old fellow looked a little better, now that he was in bed again. "But where shall we go?" he kept saying to his wife, who was fondling his hands. "Mary, where shall we go? Oh, what a lot of trouble I've brought on you. I've always been a trouble to you, always."

"No, no, you haven't," said the old woman. "It's I that's been the trouble – having that dreadful illness all those years ago, and being such an expense. You'd never have sold those secrets to pay the doctors, never have gone to prison if it hadn't been for me!" She turned to Fatty, and touched his sleeve.

"You're kind," she said. "Don't judge my old man hardly, whatever he says to you. He's paid for what he did, paid over and over again. But I was so ill, you see, and we needed money to get me better – and it was because he loved me that he did wrong."

"Don't worry about anything," said Fatty, touched by the old woman's confidence in him. "He'll soon get better in hospital. The ambulance will be here in a few minutes."

"When he came out of prison we changed our name,

you see," said Mrs. Smith, weeping again. "People point their fingers so when you've done something wrong. We tried to hide ourselves away, but always somebody found out who we were. And then kind old Mrs. Hasterley let us come here to caretake the house."

"Mrs. Hasterley!" said Fatty, surprised. "Is she still alive? She owned this place when it was The Ivies, didn't she?"

"Yes. She's an old old woman now," said Mrs. Smith. "Older than I am. You've heard of Wilfrid Hasterley, her son, haven't you – he planned the biggest diamond robbery ever heard of – and got away with it too – though nobody ever knew where he hid the diamonds. He went to prison for it, and died there – and broke his father's heart. His mother never got over it either, and she sold this house at once. My, my – every newspaper in the kingdom had a picture of this house in it then – The Ivies, it was called . . ."

"It was changed to Fairlin Hall after that, wasn't it," said Fatty, listening with great interest.

"Yes. But somehow it never got sold," said Mrs. Smith. "It had a bad name, you see. Poor Mr. Wilfrid. He had some wicked friends. He wasn't really the bad one, he was just weak and easy-going. The other two were the clever ones. One went to prison with Mr. Wilfrid – and the other was never caught. He fled away abroad somewhere – to Burma, I did hear say. Prison's a dreadful place, young sir – see what it's done to my poor old husband."

"I think I can hear the ambulance, Ern," said Fatty, raising his head. "Go and see, will you? Ask them to come as far down the drive as they can."

The old fellow opened his eyes. "Mary," he said, hoarsely. "Mary. What will you do? Where will you go?"

"I don't know, John, I don't know," said his old wife. "I'll be all right. I'll come and see you in hospital."

Ern came in at the door. "There's two men and a

stretcher," he said, importantly. "And an awfully nice nurse. The doctor couldn't come after all, but the nurse knows all about it."

A rosy-cheeked nurse looked in at the door and took everything in at a glance. "Is that my patient?" she said in a cheery voice to Mrs. Smith. "Don't you worry, dear – we'll look after him for you. Here, Potts – bring the stretcher right inside."

Everything was done very swiftly indeed. It took less than a minute to get Mr. Smith into the ambulance. He couldn't say good-bye, because he had another fit of coughing, but his old wife held his hand to the very last moment. Then the ambulance door was shut and the big van trundled up the drive and out of the gate.

"I can't pack and go tonight," said Mrs. Smith, looking dazed. "I feel queer. And I've got nowhere to go."

"Stay here tonight then," said Fatty, "I'll arrange something for you tomorrow. My mother will know what to do. But you're too upset and tired to bother about anything. The only thing is, I don't like to think of you staying here all alone at night, Mrs. Smith."

"I'll stay here with her," said Ern, suddenly. The whole affair had touched him as nothing else in his life had done. Ern longed to do something to help, he didn't care what it was – but he had Got To Do Something, as he put it to himself. And to stay and look after the sad old woman was the only thing he could think of.

"You're a good-hearted fellow, Ern," said Fatty, touched. "Thanks awfully. I was going to offer you a bed up at my house, as your uncle had sent you off – but if you'll shake down here, I'm sure Mrs. Smith would be glad."

"Oh, I would," said Mrs. Smith, and actually gave Ern, a little smile. "There's a sofa in the next room he can have. What's your name, now – Ern? That's a kind thought of yours, my boy. I'll cook you a nice little supper, you see if I don't."

"Well, I'll go home now, and see my mother, and get

her to fix up something for you, Mrs. Smith," said Fatty.

"I can work, you know," said the old lady, eagerly. "I kept this little place spotless. I can sew, too. I'll earn my keep, young sir, don't you be afraid of that."

"I'm not," said Fatty, marvelling at the brave old lady. "Now I know Ern will look after you well. Ern, what about making a pot of tea for Mrs. Smith?"

"I'll do that," said Ern. He went beaming to the door with Fatty. Then he pulled at his arm, and spoke in a low voice. "Fatty – what shall I talk to her about? To keep her from worrying, you know?"

"Well, Ern – have you got your notebook with you?" said Fatty. "What about reading her some of your poetry? I'm sure she'd like that. She'd be very surprised to think you could write poetry."

"Loveaduck! I never thought of that," said Ern, delighted. "It might keep her amused, mightn't it? So long, Fatty. See you tomorrow."

"So long, Ern – and thanks for all your help," said Fatty, making Ern beam all over his red-cheeked face. He gazed proudly after Fatty as he disappeared into the darkness of the January afternoon. Ern was absolutely certain there was no one in the whole world to equal Fatty!

Fatty surprised his mother very much when he got home, just in time for tea. He looked so serious that she was quite concerned.

"Mother, can you spare a few minutes for me to tell you something?" said Fatty. "I simply must have your help."

"Oh, Frederick dear – you haven't got into any trouble, have you?" said his mother at once.

"Not more than usual," said Fatty, with a grin that reassured his mother at once. "Listen, Mother – it's rather a long story." And he plunged into the tale of the anonymous notes, the search for ivy-covered houses, Mr. Grimble's tale, the Smiths, and Goon's treatment of them. His mother listened in amazed silence. What in the world would Frederick get mixed up in next?

Finally Fatty came to his main point. "Mother, as old Mr. Smith has gone to hospital, and Mrs. Smith's alone, and has nowhere to go, could one of your Good Causes help her?" he said. "She can do housework, and she can sew."

"Why, she can come *here*!" said his mother at once. "She can help me to make the new curtains. I'd love to have the poor old thing – and Cook's so kind she will make her really welcome in the kitchen. We're not far from the hospital too, so she can visit her husband easily, every day. She can come here, Fatty."

Fatty got up and kissed his mother. "I *knew* you'd think of something, Mother," he said. "You always do. I'm glad I own a mother like you!"

"Well, Frederick – what a nice thing to say!" said Mrs. Trotteville, pleased. "I only wish the old lady had come here tonight. I don't like to think of her there in that big empty house, all alone."

"Oh, Ern's staying there to look after her," said Fatty. "He's going to read old Mrs. Smith his poetry. Ern will have a very pleasant night, Mother!"

But he was wrong! Ern didn't have a pleasant night at all. Quite the opposite. Ern had a very disturbed night indeed!

Fatty has a Plan

"Fatty, you won't forget that you promised to fetch jumble for me from one or two of my friends, will you, for the Sale next week," said Mrs. Trotteville next day at breakfast. "I told you I'd borrowed a hand-cart for you to fetch it, didn't I?"

"Oh yes – I *had* forgotten," said Fatty. "But I'll do it, of course. You just give me the addresses and I'll see if

I've time to go today. I'm just off down to Fairlin Hall now to get old Mrs. Smith up here. I should think she could leave her bits and pieces of furniture down there, couldn't she, Mother? Just till she knows when her husband's coming out of hospital, and where they're going?"

"I don't see why not," said Mrs. Trotteville. "If old Mrs. Hasterley gave her the job of caretaking, that fat policeman has no right to turn her furniture out. If he does, tell me. I'll go and see him about it."

"Gosh – I'd like to be at the interview," said Fatty, longingly. "Are you afraid of *any*one, Mother?"

"Don't be silly, Frederick," said Mrs. Trotteville. "I'm certainly not afraid of Mr. Goon. Get a taxi for old Mrs. Smith, and bring her up here in it with her bags. Leave all the other stuff behind and lock the door. I could perhaps write to old Mrs. Hasterley, and tell her what's happened."

"Right," said Fatty, and got up. "I'll just phone for a taxi now – and tell the man to arrive at Fairlin Hall in an hour's time. That will give me time to scoot down and make sure she's ready."

"I've told Cook about her," said his mother. "And she's going to put up a bed in her room for her. Now DON'T forget about my jumble, Frederick. I've given you the addresses."

"Yes. I've got them in my pocket," said Fatty. He went out of the room and telephoned for the taxi and then fetched his bicycle. He debated whether or not to telephone to Larry and the others, to tell them the latest news, but decided he hadn't time.

He was soon cycling down to Fairlin Hall. It was a frosty morning and rather slippery, so he was careful as he rode round the corners. He hoped Goon was out on *his* bicycle too, "slipping about all over the place!" thought Fatty. "Serve him right if he fell on that big nose of his. Scaring those poor Smiths out of their lives!"

He rang his bicycle bell as he went down the drive, with Buster panting after him. He was most surprised to find the kitchen door locked when he tried to open it. Surely Ern and Mrs. Smith were up! He banged loudly on it.

Ern's face peeped cautiously from behind the window curtain, making Fatty feel still more astonished! "Come on, Ern – open the door!" he shouted. Almost at once he heard the key turned and the door opened. Ern stood there, looking pleased.

"Coo, Fatty – I'm glad you've come!" he said. "We've had such a night!"

"Whatever do you mean?" asked Fatty, surprised. "What happened?"

"Well – footsteps round the place. And someone trying to open the kitchen door. And noises, and people on the balcony, and goodness knows what," said Ern. "I was real scared. So was old Mrs. Smith. Good thing I stayed to look after her."

Fatty walked into the warm little kitchen. "Good morning, Mrs. Smith," he said, "I'm sorry you had a disturbed night."

"It was those burglars again," she said. "My old man and me, we've often heard them trying to get in. Once they did get in, too, over one of the balconies – but there's nothing to steal in this empty old place. All they took was a mirror off one of the walls in the dining-room! I was glad of Ern here, last night, I can tell you. Real brave he was."

"They did all they could to get in," said Ern. "Mrs. Smith says the house is pretty well burglar-proof now – except the kitchen part, but as she and Mr. Smith were living in these few rooms, the burglars avoided them. Not last night, though! Look, they broke this window – but they couldn't undo the catch!"

"Good thing you were here, Ern, or they might have bashed the door in, and wrecked the place," said Fatty.

"Perhaps it was tramps looking for shelter. It was a cold, bitter night."

"They went when I shouted," said Ern, proudly. "And I pretended there was a dog here, didn't I, Mrs. Smith? You should have heard me yapping. Like this!" And Ern broke into such realistic yaps that Buster looked at him, startled, and then began to bark himself.

"That was a jolly good idea, Ern, to pretend there was a dog here," said Fatty, and Ern beamed. "Well, Mrs. Smith, do you think you could get your bits and pieces together? My mother says she would be very glad if you could come and help her with her new curtains – you said you could sew, didn't you? We've put up a bed for you already."

"I never knew there were such kind folk in the world," said Mrs. Smith. "Never. I've packed already, sir. I can't do anything about my furniture. It'll have to stay here till I can send someone for it. I don't think Mrs. Hasterley will mind. I'd be glad to help your mother – if she's anything like you, it'll be a pleasure to work for her. I'll be able to see my old man, won't I, though?"

"Oh yes – the Cottage Hospital is quite near," said Fatty. "You'll be able to go every day. My mother will ring up the hospital when you arrive, and get the nurse to tell you how Mr. Smith is."

"Such kindness!" said the old lady, overcome. "And this boy Ern here – he was such a comfort last night. And the poetry he read me! Well, I reckon he's a genius, I do really."

Ern blushed. He knew he was no genius, but it was very very pleasant to be thought one! He helped Mrs. Smith out with her things, ready for the taxi. "You go with Mrs. Smith in the taxi, Ern," said Fatty. "I've got my bicycle and Buster. Go down to my shed and wait for me, when you get there. You'll find some biscuits in the tin."

"Oooh, thanks, Fatty," said Ern. He had been afraid

that he would be sent home. Perhaps he would have yet one more day with Fatty?

The taxi came, and Ern put all Mrs. Smith's things into it. He helped her in and then climbed in himself. He felt rather important. "First time I've been in a taxi!" he said. "Loveaduck, I'm getting grand!"

"I'll lock the back door and take the key," said Fatty. "I'd better return it to the house agent and I'll warn them that burglars came again."

He went back into the kitchen. It still had the Smiths' things there – rather poor bits of furniture, a carpet, worn and old, the curtains. "They could really go on a hand-cart," thought Fatty, and suddenly remembered that he had promised his mother to fetch her jumble.

He locked the door and walked to where he had left his bicycle. Then he and Buster went to the front gate. A man was standing there, hands in pocket. Buster barked at him and he kicked out.

Fatty felt rather suspicious. Why should the man be hanging about outside an empty house? Was he one of the men who had tried to break in the night before? Had he watched Mrs. Smith and Ern leaving in a taxi? Fatty rode off to the House Agent's, wondering.

He walked into the office and was relieved to find that the young and conceited Mr. Paul was not there. Only the older man was present, sitting in his corner. He recognized Fatty at once and smiled.

"I've brought you the back-door key of Fairlin Hall," said Fatty. "There were caretakers there, as you probably know, and they've left. Their furniture is still there, though."

"Well, that's nice of you," said the old clerk. "But you'd better keep the key in case the Smiths want to fetch their things. Were they given notice, or something? We haven't heard anything from Mrs. Hasterley."

"Er – Mr. Smith fell ill and has gone to hospital," said Fatty, thinking that was the best thing to say. "And by the way, burglars tried to break in there again last night."

The old clerk tut-tutted, and shook his head. "Bound to get tramps and rogues trying to get in, when a house has stood empty for years," he said. "We've tried to make it burglar proof – but what it wants is people living in it, filling the house! By the way, it's a funny thing – but some people came in to enquire about it this morning. Two men. Said they might like to buy it for a boys' prep school."

"Did you give them keys?" asked Fatty, at once.

"Yes. And I told them that a couple of old folk were there, caretaking," said the man. "I didn't know they'd gone."

Mr. Paul arrived at that moment and Fatty at once went, in case the old fellow should be admonished for wasting his time talking to him again! Fatty was very thoughtful as he rode home. People enquiring about Fairlin Hall – so soon after the Smiths had gone? Could it be someone who had tried to force a way in last night – and now, knowing that the house had no caretakers, had got the keys so that they would have the house to themselves? But what was the point of that?

"I rather think I'd better keep some kind of watch on Fairlin Hall," thought Fatty, and at once his mind flew to a possible disguise. How could he watch the house without anyone guessing?

"Of course!" he said, aloud, making the panting Buster look up at him in surprise. "Of course! I'll be a rag-and-bone man! I'll get that hand-cart, and go and collect jumble! And I'll park my cart outside Fairlin Hall, and keep my eye on anyone going in and out!"

He cycled even more quickly and went down the drive to his own house at top speed, almost running down the baker. He went straight to his shed, and found Ern there, patiently waiting.

"Ern, I'm going to disguise myself," said Fatty. "Look, you go up to the house and telephone the others. Tell them to come here at once, if they can. I'll talk to them while I'm disguising myself."

95

"Right," said Ern, thrilled, and sped off to telephone. He wasn't very sure about it, because he had rarely used the telephone – but Mrs. Trotteville, amused by Ern's serious face, got the numbers for him, and he delivered his message faithfully, saying every word so distinctly that it sounded as if he were reciting!

Meantime Fatty was swiftly disguising himself. "Dirty old rag-and-bone man," he thought. "Those old cor-duroy trousers. That torn shirt. No tie. Scarf round my neck – that filthy white one will do. Awful old boots, now where did I put them? A cap – and that frightful overcoat I found left behind a hedge one day!"

He got out his make-up box, and in ten minutes had transformed himself from a boy in his teens, to a wrinkled, dirty, slouching fellow, with protruding teeth, shaggy eyebrows and a ragged moustache.

Ern watched in unbounded admiration. "Loveaduck!" he kept saying. "Loveaduck, Fatty! How do you do it? You are a one, you are! My word, my uncle will chase you out of Peterswood, if he sees you!"

Fatty laughed. "Here come the others," he said, as Buster barked. "Let them in!" And in they all trooped – to stop in astonishment at the sight of the dirty old rag-and-bone man.

"FATTY!" squealed Bets. 'It's you! Fatty, you look *awful*! What are you going to do? Quick, tell us! What's up? Has something happened?"

Rag-a'-Bones! Rag-a'-Bones!

Everyone crowded round the dirty old rag-and-bone man, thrilled. How did Fatty do it? Except for his twink-ling eyes and too-clean hands nobody would know he was anything but what he looked!

"Your hands – and your nails, Fatty," said Bets. "Don't forget those."

"Go and fill this plant pot with some wettish earth, Bets," said Fatty, re-tying his filthy neck-scarf. "I think our gardener's out there, and if he sees me he'll chase me off the premises."

Bets rushed out with the pot and a trowel and filled it with damp earth. Fatty put his hands into it and made them really dirty. The dirt got into his nails too.

"You look simply frightful," said Larry. "And you smell a bit, Fatty. Must be that horrible overcoat."

"Yes. It does smell," said Fatty, sniffing at a sleeve. "Still, it's all in a good cause, as Mother would say. Listen, and I'll tell you quickly what's happened this morning and yesterday."

He swiftly outlined all the events, and Ern nodded in approval. That was the way to tell things – no "ers" or "ums", or stammerings – but everything set out absolutely clearly. Lovely to listen to! Everyone sat enthralled as Fatty related his tale at top speed.

"There's a few things I *can't* understand," finished Fatty, "and one is why the writer of those 'ominous' notes as Mrs. Hicks calls them, is so set on getting old Smith out – I suppose he's got some kind of spite against him – and the other is how on earth do those notes get put all over the place at old Goon's without anyone seeing them?"

"Right under my nose again, yesterday!" said Ern. "I was watching like anything, never took my eyes off the back yard, never once, not even when Fatty came into my room and spoke to me. And Mrs. Hicks was down in the kitchen too, in full view of the window – and yet there was the note, sitting on top of the plate of fish in the larder! And *neither* of us saw anyone come into the yard, or creep over to the larder window and pop the note on the fish! Beats me! Must have got an invisible cloak or something!"

"Do you know what *I* think?" said Daisy, suddenly.

"*I* think it's Mrs. Hicks who's putting the notes there! Putting them there herself! We once had a gardener who complained that someone was slipping into the garden and taking the strawberries, and there wasn't – Daddy caught *him* taking them himself! I bet it was *Mrs. Hicks* with those notes, pretending it was someone else all the time!"

There was a silence after this speech of Daisy's. Fatty stared at her – and then smacked his hand in delight on the chest beside him, making Buster jump in fright.

"*Daisy!* What an ass I've been! Of course – that's the only possible explanation! Mrs. Hicks is being paid by someone to hide those notes at Goon's – someone who doesn't want to be seen for some reason. I wonder who's paying her. Where does she live, Ern?"

"With her sister and little niece," said Ern. "To think she got me into all that trouble with my uncle! How *could* I see anyone delivering notes when all the time she must have had them hidden in her apron pocket? Just wait till I see that Mrs. Hicks again."

"No. Don't you say a word to her if you do see her," warned Fatty. "Let her think she isn't suspected at all. There won't be any more notes, of course, because old Mr. Smith has been got rid of."

"Maybe that's the end of the whole thing, then," said Pip.

"I don't think so," said Fatty. "No, I *certainly* don't think so, though Goon does, of course. There's something more behind those notes than just spite against an old man. Well, I must go. Ern, you go and see how Mrs. Hicks is getting on, and ask my mother if you can do any jobs. She'll like that."

"Can we come with you, Fatty?" asked Bets, longingly. "Could we walk a little way behind you – just to watch you being a rag-and-bone man? You do look exactly like one – in fact you look so awful that I'm sure Mother would send you off at once if you came to *our* house!"

"I say – I haven't overdone it, have I?" said Fatty, anxiously, and looked at himself in the glass. "Do these false teeth that I've put on over my own stick out too much?"

"Oh no. They're fine," said Larry. "And I love the way your shaggy eyebrows go up and down. I do hope you meet Goon."

"Well, I don't," said Fatty. "If I do I shall put on a foreign accent – or stammer or something, so that Goon can't get any sense out of me. Well, so-long. I'm going to get the hand-cart now."

He looked out of the shed window to make sure that the gardener was nowhere near, and then went rapidly to the garage. The hand-cart was there, together with a good deal of jumble taken from the attics. Fatty piled some on, and then set off to Fairlin Hall. Perhaps he could catch sight of those men who had got the keys.

He sang out the usual rag-and-bone ditty. "Rag-a'-bones! Rag-a'-bo-o-o-ones! Bring out your rag-a' bo-o-o-ones!"

He hoped that nobody would, because he hadn't much money in his pocket, and didn't really want to pay any one for jumble! He came safely to Fairlin Hall, and set down the hand-cart. He took an old pipe out of his pocket and began to fiddle with it, keeping a watch on the house, trying to make out if anyone was there.

He couldn't see anyone, and decided to wheel his cart right into the drive. Perhaps he would be able to spot the two men who had gone to the House Agent's for the keys, if he went down the drive. He decided not to shout his rag-a'-bone cry, but to go very quietly.

Ah – the men must be in the house – there was a small car at the front door. Fatty noted the number swiftly, and the make and colour. "Brown Riley, AJK 6660." Then he went on cautiously, wheeling his hand-cart, making his way to the back door.

He stood in a corner, pretending to arrange the things on the cart, but keeping his ears open for any sound that

99

might tell him where the men were, and what they were doing. He couldn't hear or see a sign of them.

He decided to go to the back door and knock, pretending that he had come to see the Smiths. But as he passed the window of the kitchen, he caught sight of a movement inside, and stopped. He peered through the window.

Two men were inside, one opening the cupboard doors, the other taking up the carpet, rolling it to one side. Fatty felt angry. What did they think they were doing? Robbing the poor old Smiths of the few things they had left behind?

Fatty went to the door and banged on it violently. There was an exclamation from inside and one of the men went to the window and peered out. He said something to the other man, and then opened the window.

Apparently he hadn't a key to open the kitchen door.

The window swung wide open, and a thin-faced elderly man looked out, and shouted at Fatty.

"What are you doing here? Clear out!"

Fatty put on a real Cockney voice. " 'Ere, mate, I've come to see me frens, the Smiffs," he said. "What you a-doin' of, messin' abart in their rooms? You ain't up to no good. I'll git the police in, see if I don't."

"The Smiths have gone," said the man, curtly. "We're probably going to buy the house; we've got the keys to look over the place. Clear out, now, your friends have gone."

"Well, what you a-doin' of then, wiv their things?" shouted Fatty. "What you rollin' up that bit of carpet for? What you . . ."

"Now, now, now, what's all this?" said a familiar voice, and to Fatty's surprise and annoyance Mr. Goon marched up to the window. "That your cart in the drive, fellow? Take it out then. And who's this in the house?"

"Constable, remove this man," said one of the men indoors. "He says he's a friend of someone called Smith, but it's my belief he knew they were gone, and came to
100

steal their bits of furniture. We've got the keys to look over the house, and suddenly saw this fellow at the back door."

"Ho! So that's it, is it?" said Goon, roughly, and turned on Fatty. "You clear orf, my man, or I'll march you off to the police-station. What's your name?"

Fatty pretended to be scared. "F-f-f-f-f," he stammered, while Goon still glared at him. "F-f-f-f-f . . ."

"Well, go on – get it out," commanded Goon, taking out his notebook. "Name *and* address."

"F-f-f-f-fred," said Fatty, "T-t-t-t-t-t . . ."

"Fred," said Goon, writing it down. "Fred what?"

"T-t-t-t-t-t," stammered Fatty, looking absolutely agonized. "T-t-t."

"All right, all right," said Goon, shutting his notebook. "I've got more important things to do than to stand here and listen to a stutterer. You go and get your tongue seen to – and take that cart out of this drive. If I set eyes on you again today I'll run you in."

"R-r-right," said Fatty, and shot out of the drive with his cart, grinning. He stood at the front gate, wondering what to do. He had seen those two men, and noted what they looked like – he had got particulars of their car – he had watched them examining the Smiths' kitchen and the things in it, goodness knew what for – and he had had a successful few minutes with Goon. What next?

He moved on down the road, shouting "Rag-a'-bones" at intervals – and then he saw someone he knew, hurrying along on the pavement.

"It's Mrs. Hicks," he thought, and his interest quickened. "I suppose she's got the morning off. Where's she going in such a hurry?"

He decided to follow her. If she had really been the one to hide those notes, then someone must have given them to her, and presumably she was being paid for hiding them at Goon's. Goon, of course, was the only person who had the power to turn the Smiths out, so that was why the notes had been sent to him. It would be very very interesting to find out who the sender was. It might throw quite a lot of light on the mystery.

Fatty trundled his hand-cart after Mrs. Hicks. Round the corner she went and round the corner went Fatty. Down a little hill and round another corner. And ah – Mrs. Hicks turned in at a gateway and vanished.

Fatty trundled his cart along the gutter, and came to a stop outside the gate. He pretended to fiddle with his pipe again, examining the house as he did so. It was a fairly big one, well-kept, and looked comfortable. From between the curtains he could see what looked like a gleaming brass ornament.

The name on the house was "KUNTAN". Who lived there? Was it someone who had given those notes to Mrs. Hicks? He decided to go to the back door and ask for anything old and done for. Even if he had to give up all his money for junk, it would be worth it, if he could find the sender of those anonymous notes.

He went cautiously down the side-entrance, and came to the back door. Beside it were piled wooden crates, with foreign words printed across them – empty crates, evidently unpacked, and then thrown out for firewood. One was already half-chopped up.

Fatty looked at them – and then one word made him stare in excitement. Just one word, stamped across each crate in big black letters – the name of the place the crate had come from.

"RANGOON"

A very lucky find

Fatty stared at the name on the crate, remembering how hard he had tried to think of a word with "goon" as part of it, when he had tried to fathom why Mr. Goon's name should have been spelt each time with a small letter g. "Mr. goon", not "Mr. Goon" had been on each of the envelopes containing those anonymous notes.

"When I asked Mother if she knew of any word with the four letters 'goon' in it, she suggested 'Rangoon'," thought Fatty, remembering. "And here's a crate with 'Rangoon' stamped across it. Can it be just chance – just a coincidence? Or is it a real clue – a clue pointing to the man who sent those letters to Goon?"

He stared at the crate again. "A man lives here who has friends in Rangoon, that's certain – friends who send him crates of something. Well, he might have Rangoon *newspapers* sent to him too – he might have cut out words and letters from them, and taken 'goon' from the title of the newspaper – *Rangoon Times*, it might be, or something like that. Gosh – I think I'm on to something here!"

He was still staring at the crate, when the back door suddenly opened and made him jump. He turned in fright, and saw Mrs. Hicks there, being ushered out by a small, foreign-looking man.

"Burmese!" thought Fatty, at once, recognizing the slanting Burmese eyes, the brown complexion and black hair. "And Rangoon is in Burma! Is this the fellow who sent those notes?"

Mrs. Hicks caught sight of him at once and frowned. "Rag-a'-bones, rubbish, jumble, anythink bought!" said Fatty at once. "Good price paid!"

"Do you want to get rid of any rubbish, sir?" asked Mrs. Hicks, turning to the Burmese. "This fellow will take it for you. Your yard looks pretty cluttered up. I can deal with him for you, if you like. What about those crates – he'd buy them for firewood – I see you've already got plenty chopped up."

"Yes, Meesees Icks," said the Burmese, and nodded. "You do beesinees wiz zis man. Much much rubbish here!"

And with that he shut the door. Mrs. Hicks beamed.

What a bit of luck! Now she could sell these crates and keep the money herself!

"You can have the crates," she said. "And I'll have a peep in the shed and see if there's any rubbish there."

She disappeared into a small shed, and Fatty followed her. It was stacked with old junk, just as his mother's attic had been – but Burmese junk! A big brass tray, green with neglect, stood on its side in one corner. A broken gong was near it, and a pair of small Burmese idols in brass. Other curiously-shaped ornaments were thrown here and there.

"You could have some of these if you liked," said Mrs. Hicks. "Cheap too -- you could sell them for a good bit to a dealer. Take what you like."

"Nobody wants junk like that," said Fatty, knowing that he must bargain. "Funny stuff, this – where's it come from? It's all foreign-like! Does it belong to that gentleman there?" and he nodded his head towards the house.

"Yes," said Mrs. Hicks. "Burmese, he is, but he married an English wife. I do sewing for her, but she's too stuck-up for me. Her husband's all right, though, and so are his two friends. Free with their money, and that's what I like."

"What are the friends like?" asked Fatty, poking about among the junk. "Burmese too?"

"No! English,,' said Mrs. Hicks. "One's been in Burma for years, but the other's a close one – don't know where he's from, I'm sure. Never opens his mouth! Well, what about this stuff? Give me a good price and you can take what you like."

"I can't sell trays and gongs," said Fatty, giving the tray a kick with his foot. "Now those crates out there – I could take some of those. And newspapers – old newspapers if you've got any. I can sell those to fishmongers and butchers. But this brass stuff – no, I wouldn't get a penny for it!"

"Go on!" said Mrs. Hicks, disbelievingly.

"Well, I'll give you sixpence for this ornament," said

Fatty, picking up a hideous little brass figure, "and six-pence each for four of those crates – and a shilling a bundle for any old newspapers you've got."

"What – a shilling for newspapers, and only sixpence for that there lovely brass ornament!" said Mrs. Hicks. "You're crazy!"

"No, I'm not. I know what I can sell and what I can't," said Fatty, fingering the ornament with his dirty hands. He looked at Mrs. Hicks from under his shaggy false eyebrows, and smiled, showing his awful protruding teeth.

"Go on, Missus. You let me buy what I can sell – four of those crates, and as many old newspapers as you've got – and one ornament."

"All right," said Mrs. Hicks. "You put four of those crates on to your barrow, while I fetch the newspapers. There's plenty stacked in the kitchen cupboard!"

Fatty grinned at her, showing his revolting false teeth again, and took the little ornament and the crates to his hand-cart. He waited here for Mrs. Hicks. Out she came with a vast number of newspapers, which she dumped in the cart.

"There you are," she said. "How much are you giving me for all that?"

"Five shillings," said Fatty. "And not a penny more."

"That's robbery," said Mrs. Hicks.

"All right, take the things back," said Fatty, and handed her a crate.

"No. Give me the five bob," said Mrs. Hicks. "But you're a robber, that's what you are." She took the five shillings, and put it into her pocket. Just as she did so, a car drew up at the house, and two men got out, the very two that Fatty had seen at Fairlin Hall! Fatty noted the car at once – aha – Brown Riley, AJK 6660. So those two men were staying here – they must be the two friends that Mrs. Hicks spoke of – one who had come from Burma, and the other whom she said "never opened his mouth." Fatty took a good look at them.

Things were beginning to fit together nicely! Rangoon. Mrs. Hicks and the notes. The two men who were staying here – was it one of them who had paid her to put the notes round and about Goon's house and yard? And now they had been to Fairlin Hall!

"They wanted to get the Smiths out because *they* want to take it – or to find something there," thought Fay, with a surge of excitement. "And what do they want to find there? Could it be – could it *possibly* be – the diamonds that were never found after the robbery? Whew! Everything's boiling up at once! My word!"

He wheeled his cart away slowly, gazing at the men as they walked up to the front door of the house. He was longing to get out his notebook, and write down their descriptions!

He set off down the road with his hand-cart, feeling quite in a daze. He suddenly caught sight of the name of a house on the other side of the road.

"Gosh! That's one of the houses that Mother asked me to collect jumble from," he thought. "Well, as I'm so near, I'd better collect it. Let's see – it was Mrs. Henry's, wasn't it."

Still in rather a daze, trying to sort out everything in his mind, Fatty pushed his hand-cart up the drive of the house. He went to the front door, quite forgetting that he was disguised as a dirty old rag-and-bone man. He rang the bell.

Mrs. Henry came to the door and stared. "The back door is round there," she said, pointing. "But we've nothing for you today. Nothing at all."

"Er – well, my mother said you'd have some old clothes, Mrs. Henry," said Fatty, politely. "For her Jumble Sale you know."

"Your *mother*," said Mrs. Henry, staring in amazement at this awful, dirty old fellow, with his shaggy grey eyebrows and filthy overcoat. "*I* don't know your mother. Who is she?"

"She's Mrs. Trotteville," said Fatty, and was most

astonished when the door was banged in his face. Then he suddenly realized that he was in disguise, and rushed off down the drive with his cart. Good gracious! How *could* he have forgotten he was a rag-and-bone man – whatever must Mrs. Henry have thought?

"*Why* did I mention Mother's name?" thought Fatty, with a groan. "She's bound to ring her up – and Mother won't be at all pleased. Well, I'll get home quickly. I'm longing to have a look through these newspapers and see if there are any from Rangoon. Mother didn't know how clever she was when she mentioned *Rangoon* to me!"

He was soon back at his house and pushed the hand-cart into the garage. He took one of the crates, with RANGOON stamped on it, and also the little brass ornament, and all the newspapers, down to his shed, keeping a sharp look-out for the gardener as he went.

The others had all gone. Not even Ern was there. "I bet they're having macaroons at the dairy again," thought Fatty, feeling suddenly hungry. "Now to have a look through these newspapers!"

He took them up one by one, and laid them down again, disappointed. "*The Daily Telegraph* – heaps of those. *The Daily Mail, Daily Express, Evening Standard* – wait now – what's this!"

He had come to a magazine, printed on cheap paper. He looked at the title. "*The Rangoon Weekly*". He scrutinized the type carefully – was it the same type as the letters and words in those notes? It really did look like it!

"I'll get that anonymous note I have, in a minute," thought Fatty. "I'll just look through a few more papers. Ah – here's another of those magazines – another *Rangoon Weekly*, but still in its wrapper. And here's another – but wait a minute, wait a minute! This one's all cut up! My word, *what* a bit of luck! I do believe this is one of the papers that the sender of those notes cut the letters from, that he stuck on to the note-paper! IT IS!"

Fatty stared at the magazine he was holding. Bits had been cut from it. The "goon" had been cut from the words *Rangoon Weekly*! Yes, not only on this page, but on the next one too! Only the "Ran" was left in the word "Rangoon" – the "goon" had been neatly snipped away!

Fatty found that his hands were trembling. The jig-saw of the mystery was fitting together now. Fatty had quite a lot of the pieces. Not many were missing! He went swiftly through the rest of the papers he had bought.

He found two more of the *Rangoon Weekly* magazines with letters and words snipped from them. He gazed at them in rapture. What a *wonderful* piece of luck!

He stood up and put the three snipped magazines into an envelope, opened a drawer and put them carefully inside. Then he locked the drawer.

"Very valuable evidence!" said Fatty. "But evidence of *what*, I don't quite know. Funny mystery this – all made up of bits and pieces – but I'll make a proper picture of them soon, and then we'll see what it shows! Whew! I wish the others were here. Oh my goodness, there's Mother calling! AND she's coming down to the shed. Whatever will she say when she sees an old rag-and-bone man here!"

Fatty reports his doings

Fatty hadn't time even to take out his horrible false teeth, before his mother opened the shed-door. She looked inside. "Frederick – are you here?"

Fatty stood with his back to her, in the darkest corner of the shed. "Yes, Mother. Did you want me?"

"Frederick, Mrs. Henry had just telephoned me," began his mother. "Do turn round, dear, I'm speaking to you . . ."

"Er – I'm in disguise, Mother," said Fatty, embarrassed.

"Turn *round*," said his mother, and Fatty reluctantly faced her. She gave a horrified scream.

"FREDERICK! Come here! Into the light. How *can* you dress like that? Disguise indeed! Oh Frederick – *don't* tell me that you were the horrible rag-and-bone man that Mrs. Henry just rang me up about. Surely, surely, you didn't really go there and say that your mother had sent you – that *I* had sent you."

"Well, Mother – it was a bit of a mistake," began Fatty, his dirty face as red as a beetroot. "I forgot I was in disguise, you see, and . . ."

"Don't talk such rubbish," said his mother, really angry. "How could you *possibly* forget you were in that horrible, revolting get-up? I'm absolutely ashamed of you, Frederick. To go to Mrs. Henry's like that! Please don't bother about collecting any more jumble for me. If you're just going to make it a joke, and deceive my friends like that, and . . ."

"But, *Mother* – I tell you I *forgot* for just a minute or two," said poor Fatty. "I'm most terribly sorry. I'll go and apologize to Mrs. Henry. You see, I'd just discovered a few amazing things, and I was a bit dazed, thinking them out, but when *you* hear what's been happening, you'll be just as astonished, and you'll . . ."

"Stop all this rigmarole," said Mrs. Trotteville, angrier than Fatty had ever seen her. "I don't wonder that Mr. Goon gets annoyed with you if you wander about like that. Has *he* seen you in that get-up too? He has? Well, I suppose he'll soon be along here then, complaining as usual. I only hope your father doesn't hear about this."

And away she went up the garden path, her skirts whisking angrily over the edges of the border. Fatty stared after her, quite shocked. *Now* he was in a fix! His mother would continue to be very upset with him – and yet he couldn't very well explain to her what had been happening. Life was going to be very uncomfortable indeed.

Fatty groaned heavily, and began to remove his make-up and various pieces of disguise. Out came the awful teeth, and off came the shaggy grey eyebrows. He stripped off the smelly overcoat and hung it up, and bit by bit became himself again.

He looked at himself in the glass. Yes, his face was clean now. Should he take the hand-cart out and go and collect the jumble his mother had asked him to? Should he go and apologize first of all to Mrs. Henry and get *her* jumble?

No, Fatty thought *not*. Let it all blow over for a day. He would sit down now and write out a report of the morning's happenings. Nothing like writing everything down, to get it straight in his mind! Fatty found his pen, and took out his notebook. He wrote rapidly.

About half-past twelve he heard the sound of voices. It was the others coming to see if he were back again. Fatty shut his notebook and went to the shed-door.

"Oh, you're back, Fatty!" said Bets, pleased. "Any luck this morning?"

"Plenty," said Fatty, grinning. "Some good and some bad."

"Oh – what was the bad?" asked Daisy, anxiously.

"Well, in a fit of absent-mindedness, I went to Mrs. Henry's front door to collect her jumble while I was in my rag-and-bone man get-up," said Fatty. "And, also absent-mindedly, I told her that my mother had sent me to her!"

There was laughter at this and horrified exclamations. "I *say* – you surely didn't say that your mother was *Mrs. Trotteville*, did you?" said Pip. "Well, *Fatty* – I never thought you could be such a prize ass! She'll telephone to your mother, and you'll get into an awful row."

"She did, and I have," said Fatty, soberly. "My mother is not on speaking terms with me now."

"Loveaduck!" said Ern. "The things you do, Fatty. What was the *good* luck?"

"Well, I've just written a sort of report on what hap-

110

pened," said Fatty. "To get things straight in my mind, really. I'll read it to you."

He opened his notebook and read from it. "Dressed up as rag-and-bone man. Went to watch Fairlin Hall. Saw car there, Brown Riley, AJK 6660. Guessed it had brought the two men who had got the keys of the place from the Agent's. Went to back door and saw men in kitchen, peering into cupboards, taking up carpets, etc. They saw me, and told me to clear out. Then Goon arrived . . ."

"Oh *no*!" said Bets. "Oh dear!"

"Goon arrived and the men told him to send me off. He asked my name, and . . ."

"Oh, you didn't give it!" cried Daisy.

"No. I said it was F-f-f-f-f," said Fatty, stammering. "T-t-t-t-t . . . well, he just couldn't be bothered with stutterers, he said, so that was all right!"

The others laughed. Fatty turned to his notebook, and went on. "I then left Fairlin Hall and went out, shouting like a rag-and-bone man. Saw Mrs. Hicks coming along in a hurry and decided to follow her. I thought she might be going to the sender of the notes, to be paid. So I followed and she went into a house called Kuntan. I went to the back door, thinking I'd ask if they'd any rubbish."

"Oh Fatty – how exciting!" said Bets. "Is this the good luck part?"

Fatty nodded, and went on reading. "Outside the door were crates with RANGOON stamped across them, evidently sent from Burma. Then the back door opened and out came Mrs. Hicks, and behind her was a Burmese – and he said she could sell me any junk she liked out of the shed. She told me she did sewing for the Burmese fellow's wife, and she also said there were two other men staying there – one from Burma, an Englishman, and another man, very quiet, that she knew nothing about."

"Two men! Were they the two you saw at Fairlin Hall, Fatty?" asked Larry.

Fatty nodded, and went on reading. "Mrs. Hicks sold

111

me a brass ornament, four of the Rangoon-stamped crates and a great bundle of newspapers. I brought them here and examined them. Among them were some magazines, printed on cheap paper, called *The Rangoon Weekly*. Three of these were cut about – letters and words had been snipped from them, especially from the word Rangoon, which, in several cases had had the four letters 'goon' cut from it."

"Fatty!" shouted Pip. "That's where the 'goon' came from on those envelopes! Gosh – fancy you getting the very papers they were cut from!"

"Sheer luck," said Fatty. "Well, there you are – we know a lot now, don't we! The only thing we *don't* know for certain is – why did those men want to turn old Smith out of Fairlin Hall? Anyone any ideas?"

"Yes. What about that diamond robbery? The diamonds were never found!" said Pip, in excitement. "Fatty, they must be hidden in Fairlin Hall somewhere! Wilfrid Hasterley must have hidden them there himself, and then gone to prison hoping that when he came out, he could get them again, and be rich!"

"Yes – and those two men you saw this morning must have been the ones who planned the robbery with him!" cried Daisy. "We know they didn't both go to prison ... one went and hid himself abroad ..."

"In Burma!" said Pip.

"And the other one, the one who was in prison with Wilfrid, must have some time been told by him that the diamonds were hidden at Fairlin Hall," said Larry. "Gosh – what a thing to happen! Fatty, what do *you* think about it all?"

"I agree with you absolutely," said Fatty. "And I'm sure that's why those fellows sent those notes about Smith to Goon, having first found out that he had a shady past. The thing is, having been away so long, they didn't know that the name of The Ivies had been changed to Fairlin Hall!"

"It all begins to fit, doesn't it," said Larry. "Gosh, to

think how we rushed round looking for ivy-covered houses! If only we'd known it was Fairlin Hall from the beginning, we could have got going much more quickly!"

"Fatty," said Bets, earnestly. "What about those hidden diamonds? Oughtn't you to tell Superintendent Jenks all this?"

"He's away up north," said Fatty. "I telephoned – only to be told to report everything to Goon! Goon, who thinks that he's settled the whole affair – why, we're still right in the very middle of it! I wish I *could* tell the Super."

"Can't you wait till he comes back, before you do anything else?" said Bets.

"What! And let those two men find the hidden diamonds!" said Ern, entering into the discussion for the first time. "Coo, Fatty – let's you and me go and hunt for them! I bet those men will be there as often as they can, searching everywhere."

"I rather think the diamonds must be in the kitchen quarters," said Fatty. "Otherwise, why try so hard to turn out the poor old Smiths?"

"I suppose the Smiths wouldn't know anything about the diamonds, would they?" said Pip. "No, of course they wouldn't. But would they know of any secret place, Fatty, do you think? You know – a trap-door leading downwards – a secret cavity in a cupboard? Mrs. Smith kept the place jolly clean, you said, and she probably knows every corner of it."

"That's quite an idea, Pip," said Fatty, considering it. "She's here, you know, helping my mother with the new curtains. I could easily have a word with her. She might let something drop that would help us. Yes, that's quite an idea. But we've got to be quick, if we're going to do any hunting ourselves, because now that the Smiths are out of the way, those two men will lose no time in getting the diamonds if they can."

"When do you think of going, then, Fatty?" asked Larry, feeling excited. "This afternoon?"

"I don't see why not," said Fatty. "I've got the back door key. Yes, let's. But we'll have to keep a good look-out for the men. Gosh, there's the lunch-gong! I must go, because I don't want my mother to be any more annoyed with me than she already is. Look – will you all be at the corner with your bikes, at three o'clock?"

"You bet!" said Pip, thrilled. "What about Ern?"

"Fatty's cook has asked me to the kitchen for dinner," said Ern, proudly. "Mrs. Smith said some nice things about me, that's why. I'll be there at three too, with Fatty."

"So long!" said Fatty, shooing them all out, and locking his shed hurriedly. "Look here, Ern, as you'll be chatting with Mrs. Smith over your dinner, you try to get a few hints about possible hiding-places, see?"

"Coo, yes, Fatty!" said Ern, delighted. "I'll do my very very best. Loveaduck – this isn't half a lark, is it!"

A disappointing afternoon

Fatty and Ern were at the corner before the others, waiting there with their bicycles. Buster was safely shut up in Fatty's bedroom.

"Well, did you enjoy your dinner, Ern?" asked Fatty.

"Oooh yes," said Ern happily. "Made quite a fuss of me they did. Especially Mrs. Smith. She told your cook and Jane all about my portry."

"You don't mean to say you read them any?" said Fatty, amused. Ern went red.

"Well – they kept on and on about it," he said. "So I read them one or two pomes. They liked the one about the Ivies, Fatty – but I told them you wrote half of it. I wasn't going to let them think I'd written those *good* lines. Coo, Fatty, I don't know how you let your tongue go loose, like you say, and spout out portry by the yard, rhymes and all."

"You do it like this, Ern, as I've told you before," said Fatty, and rested his bicycle against the fence. He stood up and opened his mouth. Ern waited breathlessly. Fatty began to declaim at top speed.

> *"Oh every time*
> *You want a rhyme,*
> *Then let your tongue go loose,*
> *Don't hold it tight,*
> *Or try to bite,*
> *That won't be any use!*
> *Just let it go*
> *And words will flow*
> *From off your eager tongue,*
> *And rhymes and all*
> *Will lightly fall*
> *To make a little song!"*

"There you are, Ern, that's how you do it," said Fatty, with a chuckle. "You try it when you're alone. Just think of the first line, that's all – then let your tongue go loose."

"I don't think I've got your sort of tongue," sighed Ern, half-inclined to try it there and then. "Coo, Fatty, it's queer, you know – you don't really care about writing portry, and I do, but I can't. And *I'd* give anything to write it, and you wouldn't, but you can."

"You're muddling me, Ern," said Fatty. "Ah, here are the others. Good."

Soon all six of them were cycling to Fairlin Hall. They sent Ern in to make sure the coast was clear. He came back very quickly.

"Okay!" he said. "No car at the front door. Nobody about at all, as far as I can see."

"Come on, then," said Fatty. "We'll hide our bikes in some thick bushes round the back, so that they can't be seen. We'll take it in turns to keep a watch out. Pip, you keep first watch."

115

"Right," said Pip, at once, though he was longing to go in with the others. "If you hear me whistling 'Over the Seas to Skye', you'll know there's something up."

They put their bicycles behind a thickly-growing bush and went to the kitchen door. Fatty unlocked it, and looked round. "I think we'll keep to the kitchen quarters," he said. "Let's see – there's the kitchen – a small scullery – and a room the Smiths had for a bedroom. Oh, and there's a tiny bathroom here as well, leading off the bedroom."

"Where exactly do we look?" asked Bets. "I've been trying to think where I'd hide diamonds away in these rooms, if I had to – and except for silly places like at the back of a drawer, or on the very top of a cupboard, I can't think of any."

"Well – the hiding-place is sure to be pretty good," said Fatty. "A prepared one, perhaps – you know, a hole knocked in the wall behind a cupboard, and then the cupboard put back again."

"Oh," said Bets. "Well, I'm pretty sure I shouldn't find *that*."

The five began to hunt carefully. Every mat, every scrap of carpet was turned back. Every bit of furniture was moved. Then Bets went to a chest of drawers.

"No good looking in the drawers of that chest, Bets, old thing," said Fatty. "The furniture belongs to the Smiths, you know. Hallo, what's this?"

Everyone turned at once. Fatty was down on his knees, trying to peer into a hole that was at the bottom of one corner of the kitchen wall. "It seems to go back a little way," he said. "Gosh, I can see something there! Bets, can you get your tiny hand in and feel?"

Bets knelt down and tried to put her hand in at the hole. "I can feel something!" she said excitedly. She stretched her fingers to the utmost and tried to get hold of whatever it was, with the very ends of her fingers. There was a sudden SNAP! and Bets screamed.

"Oh! My finger! Something caught it!"

116

"It's a mouse-trap, isn't it!" said Larry, with a squeal of laughter. "I know that SNAP! Mother put a trap in my bedroom last night, and it went SNAP and caught a mouse."

'Oh, Bets – did it trap your fingers?" said Fatty, in concern, as Bets stood up, squeezing the fingers of her right hand.

"No. Not quite. The trap just missed them," said Bets. "Oh, Fatty – and I thought I was reaching out for a bag of diamonds! and it was only just a mouse-trap that the Smiths must have put into the hole!"

Fatty took his torch from his pocket and bent down to make sure, his cheek against the ground, as he flashed the light of his torch into the hole. "You're right, Bets," he said. "It's a trap. What a disappointment. Still – a bag of diamonds wouldn't be pushed into a mouse-hole, of course! The hiding-place will be very much cleverer than that! Call Pip in, Ern, and take his place."

Pip came in, rubbing his hands. "Jolly cold out there," he said, stamping his feet. "Shouldn't be surprised if it's going to snow. Found anything?"

"Not a thing," said Bets. "Except a mouse-trap."

The hunt was a complete failure. Fatty gave it up after a whole hour's search. It was getting dark, and he was the only one with a torch.

"No go," said Fatty. "I think probably only professional police searchers could find the diamonds. They may even be embedded in one of the walls – a hole could have been made, the plaster put back, and painted over. Short of pulling the walls to pieces, and taking up the floor, I don't see that we can do anything else! I vote we go and have tea somewhere."

"You can come and have it at our house," said Pip. "Mother's gone out, and she said if we cleared away ourselves and washed up, she would leave a smashing tea on the table. And if we break anything, we've got to replace it."

"Jolly nice of your mother," said Larry. "Shall we go to Pip's, Fatty?"

"Yes. Splendid idea," said Fatty. "I'd have liked you all to come to my house for tea, but Mother is Very Very Distant to me at the moment. I really might be some third cousin she hasn't seen for years, and doesn't want to know. Poor Mother – she'll never get over my going to Mrs. Henry's disguised as a smelly rag-and-bone man. That overcoat did smell, you know."

"My word it did," said Pip. "You smell of it a bit still, Fatty. Ern, you can come to tea, too, of course."

Ern beamed. He had been afraid that he might not be asked. What would Sid and Perce say when he told them how he'd been here, there and everywhere? He was very happy indeed as he cycled up to Pip's with the others – but quite horrified when he suddenly met his uncle round the corner! Goon saw him at once and leapt off his bicycle. He caught hold of Ern's handle-bars and Ern wobbled and fell off.

"What you doing here in Peterswood, Ern?" he demanded. "Didn't I tell you to go home? What you been doing all this time?"

"I asked him to stay with me," said Fatty, in what Goon called his "high and mighty voice." "Don't you want to know what happened to those poor old Smiths, Mr. Goon – the ones you tried to turn out of their care-taking job?"

"All I know is they've gone, and good riddance to them," said Goon. "Smith was a traitor – didn't ought to be in any responsible job. The man that wrote those notes to warn me, was quite right."

"Well, Mrs. Smith is staying up at our house, helping my mother," said Fatty. "And Mr. Smith is in the cottage hospital, very ill, but Mrs. Smith can see him every day, you'll be pleased to know. At least I hope you *will* be pleased to know. You were very unkind to her, Goon."

"Don't you talk to me like that, you – you pest of a boy!" said Goon, furious at being ticked off by Fatty in front of Ern, whose eyes were nearly falling out of his

118

head. "And let me tell you this – Fairlin Hall's bin bought, see – and anyone going there will be TRESPASSING, and will be PROSECUTED. Those are the new owner's orders. Two gentlemen have bought it – very nice too, they are, and very friendly. So you be careful, Master Frederick Trotteville."

"Thank you for the news, Goon," said Fatty. "I was rather expecting it. But why should you think I'd want to go there?"

"Oh, I wouldn't put it past you to go and move out all the Smith's furniture," said Goon. "Always interfering in everything! Ern, you come with me."

"I've been asked out to tea, Uncle," said Ern, edging away. He leapt suddenly on his bicycle and rode away at top speed.

"Gah!" said Goon, in disgust. "You've made Ern as bad as you are. Just wait till I get my hands on him!"

Goon rode away angrily. That Frederick Trotteville! Was he up to anything? Goon couldn't help feeling that there was still something going on that he didn't know about. Gah!

The others laughed and rode off again. They arrived at Pip's to find Ern waiting for them behind a bush. Soon they were sitting round a loaded tea-table. Fatty wished he had gone to fetch Buster, because Mrs. Hilton, Pip's mother, had left a plate of dog-biscuits for him, smeared with potted meat, a meal that old Buster simply loved!

"Will the Smiths be able to get their furniture out before those men move in?" asked Ern. "Mrs. Smith was very worried about it at dinner-time. And she said that lots of things ought to be done before anyone else uses that kitchen. She said the kitchen-range was right down dangerous. And she said the sink smelt something awful. I did try to find out if there were any possible hiding-places, Fatty – but the only things she said were about the kitchen-range, and the sink, and the coal-cellar, and the cold pipe in the bathroom, and the mouse-hole in the wall."

"What did she say about the coal-cellar?" asked Fatty. "We never examined that, now I come to think of it."

"She said the steps down were so rickety she was afraid of breaking her leg," said Ern. "And she said the cold pipe in the bathroom ran so slowly that their baths were always too hot. It had a leak too, she said, and the sink . . ."

"Smelt something awful," said Fatty. "Hm. Nothing very helpful there – though I think we *ought* to have looked in the coal-cellar. I've a good mind to go there tonight, as a matter of fact. It'll be my only chance if those men are going to move in. Yes, I think I *ought* to have a squint at that coal-cellar."

"I'll come with you, Fatty," said Ern, eagerly. "Do say I can."

"No," said Fatty. "I shall go alone, if I do go, but I'm not certain yet. If only Superintendent Jenks was back I'd go and see him, and ask for a couple of men to search those kitchen quarters. No, no more jam tarts, thank you, Pip! Ern, you'll go pop if you have any more. Try Buster's dog-biscuits smeared with potted meat!"

"Well, they don't look half bad," said Ern, and made everyone laugh. "I've a good mind to try one!"

There wasn't much left on the table when they had all finished. "Let's play cards now, Fatty," said Pip. But Fatty shook his head.

"No. I want to go to the flower-shop before it shuts," he said.

"Why? To buy another Coleus plant?" said Bets, with a laugh.

"No – to buy a very expensive bunch of red roses for someone I've mortally offended," said Fatty, solemnly. "My mother! I simply cannot bear to go home and be treated like a bad smell – and Mother really is Very Very Annoyed with me. I feel rather bad about it, actually, she's such a dear. See you tomorrow! Mind you don't break anything when you wash up!"

Fatty Investigates

Ern had been told that he could sleep the night in Fatty's shed, if he didn't want to go home. He decided that he certainly would – and Ern had a very strong reason for his decision.

If Fatty was going down to Fairlin Hall that night, then he, Ern, was going too. Not *with* Fatty, because he might be sent back. He was just going to follow him, and make sure nothing happened to him.

"Just suppose those men have moved in," thought Ern, anxiously. "Fatty would be no match for them. I won't let him see me – but I'll keep watch, in case those men are there and hear him."

So, as he cycled back to Fatty's after Pip's tea-party, Ern made his plans. He would leave his bicycle in a bush down the drive, at Fatty's house, so that as soon as Fatty went off, he could follow him. And if Fatty walked, well, Ern would walk too. He felt in his pocket to see if his torch was there. Yes, it was.

Fatty was down in his shed when Ern arrived, looking through his notes. "Hallo, Ern!" he said. "Did you break anything when you all washed up?"

"Not a thing," said Ern. "You ought to have stayed, Fatty. We played cards, and little Bets won the lot. Did you get some flowers for your mother?"

"I did," said Fatty. "And Mother was very pleased. So that's settled. I'm not a nasty smell any more."

"Are you really going down to Fairlin Hall tonight, Fatty?" asked Ern.

"I am – and you are *not* coming, so don't ask me again," said Fatty. "I shall creep down the stairs when the household is in bed. Ern, if you're sleeping down in

121

this shed, I think you'd better have Buster, if you don't mind. He might bark the place down if I go without him."

"Oooh, I will. I'd like to," said Ern, who was very fond of the lively little Scottie. "He'll be company."

"Well, I must go in and make myself respectable," said Fatty. "They're expecting you to supper in the kitchen, Ern. You'd better write a bit more poetry to recite to them."

"Oooh, I couldn't write it in such a hurry," said Ern. "It takes me weeks to write two lines, Fatty."

"Rubbish," said Fatty. "Remember what I told you. Just let your tongue go loose, and it comes – it comes! Think of a good line to begin with, Ern – then let your tongue wag away as it likes."

Fatty left him, and Ern opened his notebook. He looked at his "portry". If only he could think of it easily, like Fatty! It would be so very very nice to stand up in the kitchen tonight and recite a new "pome".

"Well, I'll have another try," said Ern, valiantly, and stood up. He worked his tongue about a little to get it "loose" and then delivered himself of one line.

"There was a pore old mouse . . ."

He waggled his tongue desperately, hoping the next line would come spouting forth, just as it did when Fatty made up verses. "There was a pore old mouse . . . mouse. There was a pore old mouse . . ."

"Snogood," said Ern, flopping down again. "Fatty's tongue must be different from mine. I wonder what's for supper tonight."

At ten o'clock Fatty said good night to his mother and father and went up to bed. He waited for half an hour and then he heard his parents come up, and the lights click off. He quickly put on his overcoat and slipped downstairs again, with a very quiet Buster at his heels. Buster's tail was wagging hard. A walk! At this time of night too!

It was snowing a little as Fatty walked down to his shed. He knocked quietly. Ern opened the door at once.

"Goodness – aren't you going to get undressed, Ern?" said Fatty, in surprise. "I left you an old pair of pyjamas, didn't I?"

"I'm not sleepy yet," said Ern, truthfully. "Hullo, Buster. Come on in. Well, good luck, Fatty."

"Thanks. I'll be off," said Fatty, and went down the path, the snowflakes shining white in the light of his torch. Ern waited a few seconds and then slipped out himself, pulling on his overcoat. Buster began to bark frantically as Ern shut the door. He leapt up and down at it, flinging himself against it. He was furious at being deserted by both Fatty *and* Ern.

"Blow!" thought Ern. "I hope he won't wake everyone. Still, the shed's pretty far away from the house!"

He hurried along down the garden-path, into the drive and out of the front gate. He could just see Fatty passing under a street-lamp some way off. He followed quickly, his feet making no noise on the snow-covered path.

Fatty had no idea that Ern was following him. He went along quickly, feeling the key of the kitchen door of Fairlin Hall in his pocket. His mind went over what Ern had related to him. Kitchen-range. Smelly sink. Leaking pipe. Coal-cellar. Yes – he'd certainly better examine that coal-cellar. It might make a splendid hiding-place.

Behind him plodded Ern. Fatty came to the drive of Fairlin Hall and turned down it cautiously, looking for lights in the house. Ern turned in after him, keeping Fatty in sight as best he could, a dark shadow in the distance.

Fatty could see no lights anywhere, but of course the electricity would not be connected yet. If the two men came, they would have to use torches. The Smiths had had an oil lamp in their kitchen, because no gas or electricity was on.

"Those men will have to come pretty soon, certainly within the next week, I suppose," thought Fatty. "I don't expect they *really* mean to buy it – all they want is to find the hoard of diamonds they stole so many years ago, and take them. Anyway, they've got the keys, so they can get in at any time."

He let himself in quietly at the kitchen door, and left it open, in case he had to run out quickly. He slipped through the scullery and kitchen, and went to the door that led from the kitchen to the hall. He opened it and stood there listening. He could hear nothing at all.

Slipping off his shoes he padded into the dark hall and went to the bottom of the stairs. There was no light to be seen anywhere, and the whole house was heavy with silence. "Almost as if it were listening, too!" thought Fatty. "Well, as there's absolutely no one about, I'll just examine that coal-cellar. I suppose it's outside, because I don't remember seeing a cellar indoors."

He put on his shoes again and slipped through the kitchen and out into the little yard. He didn't see Ern standing like a statue in the shadow of some bushes not far off; but Ern saw the light from Fatty's torch, and knew that he was going to examine the coal-cellar.

The Fairlin Hall coal-cellar was a truly enormous one. A large, heavy grating covered the entrance hole, and Fatty lifted it off, and peered down. A steep wooden ladder led downwards to what looked more like an underground room than a coal-hole. The ladder was rickety, as Mrs. Smith had related to Ern, and Fatty didn't really fancy going down it.

He flashed his torch down the ladder, and came to the conclusion that if any diamonds had been hidden in the cellar they would have been discovered, for there was very very little coal left – only a sprinkling over the stone floor.

Fatty went back to the house, and flashed his torch over the kitchen-range. Was there any hiding-place at the back? No, not possibly. He went round the rooms methodically, trying to think of somewhere he hadn't examined that afternoon.

He suddenly heard a small sound, and stood still, listening. There it was again. What was it?

Was it someone opening the front door and shutting it? Fatty's heart began to thump a little. If it were the two men, they would probably come into the kitchen quarters to search. He switched off his torch and stood in the tiny bathroom listening intently.

Suddenly he felt a soft touch on the top of his head, and he stiffened in fright. It felt like a moth settling on his hair – but no moths were about in January.

There it was again – just a soft touch on his hair. Fatty put up his hand and felt the spot – and it was damp! He heaved a sigh of relief. Just a little drip of water from somewhere – probably from the leaking water-pipe that Mrs. Smith had told Ern about!

He stood there in the dark, listening for any further sound, but none came. He must have been mistaken. He took a step forward and switched on his torch again, looking up at the water-pipe to see where the drip had come from.

"It's from that loose joint," thought Fatty, seeing a place where two pipes had been joined together. "Gosh, it made me jump."

He reached up his hand and touched the joint. It was rather loose, so no wonder the water leaked out. A sudden idea flashed into Fatty's mind – an idea that made him catch his breath. Could it be – no, it *couldn't* be what he was thinking!

His hand shook a little as he held the torch up to the joint of the pipes. Why should there be a join there, held together by an iron band round the pipe? Could the pipe have been deliberately cut – could something have been slid into it – then the cut ends fixed together by the joint, hiding whatever had been forced into the pipe?

Fatty stood below the narrow little pipe, hearing the small noise that the tiny drip made every now and again. Mrs. Smith had said that the flow in the cold water-pipe was very poor – very slow – so slow that they couldn't make their hot baths cool! Was that because the pipe had been stuffed with something that impeded the flow of the water – stuffed with *diamonds*, perhaps!

Fatty flashed his torch on the joint again. It didn't look as neat a job as the other joints he could see. A surge of excitement made his heart begin to beat fast.

"I believe I've got it!" thought Fatty to himself. "I really believe I have! My word – if Wilfrid Hasterley really did push all his diamonds into a water-pipe and then sealed it up, he was a wizard at hiding things! I bet he put a few big ones in first, hoping they would jam together, and not be taken down to the outlet. Whew!"

He had heard no more noises, and felt certain he was mistaken in thinking anyone had come into the house. He would surely have heard something more by now! He debated whether he should find the main water-cock and turn off the water. Then he might be able to hack off the pipe-joint, force the two ends of the little pipe apart, and peer into them.

But where *was* the water-cock? He hadn't the faintest idea. "No good messing about," thought Fatty. "I'll get back home – and tomorrow I simply MUST get into touch with the Superintendent, even if I have to telephone to the back of beyond!"

He crept silently out of the little bathroom, shining his torch in front of him – and then he had the shock of his life! Someone pounced on him from a corner and gripped him so tightly that he couldn't even struggle!

Then a torch was shone into his face, and a voice exclaimed: "Oh – so it's that fat boy, is it? Why are you here again? What are you looking for? Go on, tell us, or we'll make you!"

Fatty saw two men – yes, the two he had been on guard against, and listening for! So he *had* heard something! What an ass he had been not to go and investigate.

He began to shout at the top of his voice. "Let me go! Let me go! Help! Let me go!"

"There's nobody to hear you!" said one of the men. "Shout all you like! Go on – shout!"

126

Ern has a really exciting time!

But there *was* somebody to hear Fatty, of course. Ern was still outside, shivering in the shelter of the bush he was hiding in. He almost jumped out of his skin when he heard Fatty's shouts.

"They've got him – somebody in the house has caught him!" thought Ern, shaking at the knees. "What shall I do? I daren't go in – I'll be caught too if I do. Oh Fatty – what can I do to help?"

He stole from the shelter of his bush and crept nearer to the kitchen door. He could hear a struggle going on as Fatty tried to kick the men on the shins. He heard Fatty yell in pain at some blow given him.

"You let me go! Oh! You brute! Let go!"

Ern listened in anguish. He longed to go to Fatty's help, but what *would* be the sense of two of them being caught? Oh, poor Fatty! Ern strained his ears to hear what the men were saying.

"Lock him in this cupboard," panted one of them. "My word, he's strong. Knock him over the head."

"No. Be careful. I don't want a spell in prison again," said the second man. "Shove him in!"

Ern heard a crash as Fatty was pushed violently into the big cupboard, where the Smith's brooms and brushes and pans still stood. Then there was a short silence. Not another sound from Fatty!

"Lock the door on him," said a voice. "He's knocked out for a bit, at any rate. My word, he gave me a kick that almost took off my knee-cap! Now come on – we've *got* to find those stones! We know they're here somewhere!"

Ern, his heart thumping so loudly that he felt the men

must hear it, stood watching their torches flashing here and there, as they made their search for the hidden diamond haul. There was no sound to be heard from Fatty, not even a groan. Ern began to feel very anxious.

"I must get help!" he thought. "I really must. But how?" He stood and thought hard.

"I'll go and stand at the front gate and stop the first person coming by," he decided at last, and he crept through the falling snow up to the gate. He waited, shivering, for a few minutes, and then, to his delight, saw someone coming. It was a small man, hurrying along. Ern ran to him.

"Please will you help! Two men have got hold of a friend of mine in that empty house there. They've hurt him and locked him in a cupboard. Please come and help him."

The little man looked quite scared. "That's a matter for the police!" he said.

"Oh *no*!" said Ern, thinking of his uncle at once. "No, I don't want the police here."

"Well, all I can do is to telephone them for you," said the man, and hurried off. "It's the police you need!"

Ern was in despair. The last person he wanted to see was his uncle, the very *last*! He hurried back to the house, his feet making no noise over the snow. He peeped through the kitchen window. No sign or sound of poor old Fatty – but the men were obviously still there, for Ern could see the flash of their torches from the little bedroom.

He debated whether he dared to go in and unlock the cupboard door. No, he daren't. He couldn't possibly get Fatty out without making a noise. Ern's heart sank down into his shoes. "I'm no good when there's trouble about," he thought, sorrowfully. "No good at all. Fatty would know what to do at once. I wish I had better brains."

And then he jumped violently as something brushed against his leg, and then planted a wet lick on his hand.

128

"Oooh! What's that! Oh, it's *you*, Buster! Sh! How in the world did you get out?"

Buster wagged his tail. He knew quite well how he had got out! He had leapt up on to the chest of drawers in Fatty's shed, and had found the window open a little. He had squeezed himself through the opening and jumped to the ground. Then he had nosed his way after Ern's tracks and Fatty's, sniffing them easily all along the roads to Fairlin Hall.

But now Buster sensed trouble, and that was why he hadn't barked when he saw Ern! He put his paws up on the boy's knees and whined a very small whine, as if to say, "Where's Fatty? Please tell me what's up?"

Then Buster heard the men inside the house and his ears pricked up at once. He ran to the door. He smelt Fatty's tracks, he smelt Fatty himself! Where was his master? What had happened to him? He ran to the cupboard and pawed at it. He knew Fatty was in there!

The men heard him and ran out of the bedroom. They flashed their torches on the little Scottie – and at the same moment he leapt at them. One man felt a nip on his ankle – then the other felt a glancing bite on his hand. He hit out at the excited dog, who bounded all round them like a mad thing, barking, and nipping them whenever he could.

One man ran out of the kitchen into the hall, and the other followed. Buster went too, and Ern heard him chasing them all the way up the stairs. Ern was almost weeping in relief. He raced to the locked cupboard and turned the key.

"Fatty! Quick! Come out!" he said.

Fatty was lying back on a collection of pails, pans and brushes. He stared up at Ern, still half-dazed.

"Ern!" he said, in a weak voice. "What's up?"

"Oh Fatty – you've an awful bruise on your head," said Ern, in distress. "Quick, I want to get you out of here. Can you stand? Let me help you."

Fatty stood up with difficulty. Evidently the blow on

his head had quite dazed him. Ern helped him anxiously out into the air.

"Let me sit down," said Fatty. "This cold air is making me feel better. I don't feel quite so dazed. Gosh, what happened? I'm just remembering! Ern, what on earth are *you* doing here? And is that Buster I can hear barking?"

"Fatty, don't bother about anything now," said Ern, as the boy sat down heavily beside a bush. "Old Buster is chasing the men who knocked you out. Stay here a minute and I'll just go and see what's happened to him."

Ern went back cautiously to the kitchen. But before he could even look inside, he saw a lamp coming waveringly round the corner of the house, and stared at it in amazement. Who was this coming now? Then a loud and angry voice hailed him.

"ERN! What you doing here? Some fellow phoned me and said there was a boy here who wanted help – Ern, if it was *you* playing a joke like that on me, I'll – I'll . . ."

It was Goon! He leapt off his bicycle and strode towards the terrified Ern, who promptly fled into the kitchen. Goon padded after him, quite convinced that Ern had got him out here in the snowy night just for fun.

And then Buster appeared at top speed! He had heard Goon's voice, and had come to investigate. He leapt at the policeman in delight and nipped his trousers at the ankle.

"What – that dog's here too! Is that fat boy here as well?" thundered Goon. "What's going on? I never heard of such doings in my life. Oh get off, you horrible little dog! Clear orf, I say! Ern, get him off, or I'll pull every hair out of your head! WILL you get away, dog?"

But Buster was having the time of his life. No Fatty to call him off, nobody to stop him from harrying his old enemy all he liked. It was too good to be true! He chased Mr. Goon all round the kitchen, and then into the broom cupboard, where the angry policeman subsided among the same pails and brooms that Fatty had fallen on.

And then Ern suddenly saw the two men peeping round the door, and he crouched in a corner in terror, praying that they would not see him. One flashed his torch into the cupboard and saw the policeman there, with Buster on top of him.

"Look there – the police!" he cried in alarm, and slammed the cupboard door at once. He turned the key, locking the door. "Well, thank goodness we've got rid of the dog, and locked up the policeman," he said, in a shaky voice. "I can't understand all this. Where's that boy gone that we knocked out?"

"He's lying under the bobby, I expect," said the second man. "He was quite knocked out. The policeman must have fallen on top of him, trying to get away from that vicious little dog. Phew! What a night! Do we search any more – or what?"

"No. We get back to Kuntan," said the second man. "My ankles are bitten all over! I must put some iodine on them. I'd like to have killed that dog!"

"Well, he can keep the policeman and the boy company till morning," said his companion. Then he turned sharply, "Hallo – who's this?" he said, and he flashed his torch on to the corner where Ern was crouching.

And then Ern behaved magnificently. He reached up a hand and swept a whole row of kettles and pans off the shelf just above him. They clattered to the floor with an awful din, and startled the two men out of their wits. Then Ern leapt up into the air, hands above his head, and moaned in a horrible, hollow voice, "I'm coming! I'm coming!"

The two men took to their heels and raced out of the kitchen door. This was absolutely the last straw – what with boys and policemen and dogs roaming about – and now this awful creature, whatever it was, clattering pans everywhere! The men were really terrified.

Ern looked out of the door after them, hardly able to

believe that his sudden mad idea had acted so well. Then he heard a loud shriek, and wondered what had happened. Then came a crash, and angry voices.

"What's up now?" wondered Ern, uneasily. As the voices came no nearer he tiptoed out of the kitchen door and went cautiously towards them.

"Coo – loveaduck! They've fallen down the coal-cellar!" he said. "Fatty must have forgotten to put the grating back over it – and down they've gone! They must be hurt or they'd try getting up the ladder. Quick, Ern, my lad, you can do something here!"

And Ern flew to where the big heavy grating lay on the snow-covered ground. He dragged and pulled, pulled and dragged, panting hard. At last he got it half across the cellar-opening, and the men, who had been quite silent, hoping that perhaps there hiding-place would not be discovered, suddenly realized what was happening.

One gave a yell and began to climb the ladder – but the rickety rungs broke under his weight and he fell back into the cellar again. Ern at last pulled the grating right across. Then he flashed his torch down at the two angry, frightened men.

"You can stay there till you're fetched!" he said, and looked about for something else heavy enough to drag over the grating, to keep it down. He found the dustbin, and dragged it there, and then filled it with stones from a nearby rockery. He was very hot and tired when he had finished. The men yelled and threatened him with all kinds of terrible things – but Ern was feeling on top of the world, and took no notice.

"Loveaduck – there's the men down the coal-cellar – and uncle in the cupboard with Buster on top of him – I've done a good night's work," thought Ern, hurrying back to where he had left Fatty. "If only poor old Fatty is feeling better!"

Fatty was decidedly better. He was standing up wondering whether to go and join the row he could hear going on not far off. He didn't know that it was Ern well and truly imprisoning the men in the coal-cellar!

"Hallo, Fatty," said Ern's voice. "You better? Come on, I'll take you home. You lean on me. No, don't ask any questions now – you'll be all right tomorrow. I'll answer them then."

And so the still-dazed Fatty, frowning with an enormous headache, went slowly home, leaning on Ern's shoulder. His head was in a muddle. All he wanted was to lie down and rest in bed. Good old Ern – he'd explain everything to him tomorrow! Fatty simply couldn't be bothered to worry about anything just then!

A most surprising finish

Ern slept the night in Fatty's room, so that if the boy wanted anything in the night he could get it for him. He curled himself up in a chair, dressed as he was, meaning to keep awake and think over the exciting happenings of the night. Coo – think of Uncle in that cupboard with Buster barking in his ear. A very very pleasant thought for Ern!

He fell asleep – and as for Fatty, once his headache had eased, he too slept like a log. He sat up in bed at half-past seven next morning as lively as a cricket, and was most amazed to see Ern asleep in his arm-chair. His mind groped back to the evening before. What had happened?

"I can remember as far as being attacked by those men – and being thrown into the cupboard – but all the rest is hazy," thought Fatty, and gently felt the bump on his head. "I suppose they knocked me out. How did I get here? Ern! Wake up, Ern!"

Ern awoke with a jump and uncurled himself. He went

to Fatty's bed. "Coo, Fatty – you've got an awful bruise on your head," he said. "How do you feel?"

"Fine," said Fatty, getting out of bed. "Ern, how did I get back here? What on earth happened last night? How did *you* come into it? You weren't even there!"

"Oh yes I was, Fatty," said Ern. "You just listen. Get back into bed and I'll tell you the best story you ever heard in your life."

"Well, make it short," said Fatty. "I've simply *got* to phone the Superintendent now!"

"Yes, you have. But there's no hurry," said Ern, grinning. "I've got everyone nicely in the bag for you."

"What do you mean, young Ern?" demanded Fatty. "Don't sit there grinning – tell me everything."

"Well – my uncle's locked up in the cupboard where *you* were," said Ern, "and Buster's with him, and the two men are imprisoned in the coal-cellar. I scared them and they ran out and didn't see the opening – and fell down it. Good thing you didn't put the grating back, Fatty. I pulled it across the hole, and my word, it was heavy, and I stood the dustbin on top as well and filled it with big stones from the rockery."

Fatty was too astonished to say a word. He stared at Ern as if he couldn't believe his ears. "Is this true?" he said at last. "How was it you were there?"

"I followed you," said Ern. "I was afraid something might happen to you. I left Buster in the shed, but he must have got out somehow. He chased those men all over the place."

"Ern – thank you," said Fatty. "Thank you more than I can say. I made a mess of things – and you didn't. You – you did magnificently. My word, Ern, what a time you had!"

"Coo, I did!" said Ern. "I dragged you out of that cupboard, Fatty, and put you outside in the drive – you did look awful. I was that upset and scared. Then suddenly I wasn't scared any more, and, well – I suppose I sort of went mad, and swept all the pans off the shelf,

134

clitter-clatter, and booed at those men at the top of my voice, and chased them!" Ern began to laugh as he remembered. "Honest, I didn't know I could do it."

"You'll have to write a poem about it, Ern," said Fatty, getting out of bed again. "Well, I can see there's a lot of loose ends to tie up this morning! My word – fancy old Goon having to spend the night in a cupboard with Buster – I bet he didn't enjoy that."

Fatty was soon very busy indeed. He felt perfectly all right now, though the bruise on his head was sore. He telephoned immediately to the Superintendent's office, and oh, what a relief, he was there! Fatty was put through to him at once.

"This is an early call, Frederick," said the Superintendent's crisp voice. "What's up?"

"Plenty," said Fatty. "Superintendent, will you turn up details of a big diamond robbery over twenty years ago, when a Wilfrid Hasterley of The Ivies, Peterswood, and two friends, got away with an enormous haul of diamonds."

"I don't need to turn it up," said the Superintendent. "I was a young man then, and happened to be one of the men put on the job. Wilfrid got a jail sentence and died in prison. One man fled abroad, and we never heard of him again. The other man went to jail, and came out a few months ago. We meant to watch him, hoping he'd know where Wilfrid had hidden the diamonds, but he was too wily and went to ground. What about it? It's a very old case now."

"I know. But two of the men came back to Peterswood – to The Ivies, which is now called Fairlin Hall," said Fatty. "And . . ."

"Frederick! You don't mean this!" said the Superintendent's voice, sounding amazed. "Where are they?"

"Well, at the moment they're imprisoned in a coalcellar at Fairlin Hall," said Fatty, chuckling. "And you'll be surprised to know that that was the work of young Ern, Superintendent – Goon's nephew, you know."

"Good heavens!" said the Superintendent, sounding more astonished than ever. "What about Goon? Is he in on this too?"

"Well – he was at the beginning," said Fatty. "But he didn't last till the end, I fear. He gave up half-way. At the moment, I regret to say, he's locked up in a broom cupboard at Fairlin Hall, with Buster. He's been there all night."

There was a dead silence, then the Superintendent spoke again. "This isn't a joke, is it, Frederick?" he said.

"Oh no. It's all absolutely true," said Fatty, earnestly. "Can you come over? We could go down to Fairlin Hall and you can examine the various people there who are imprisoned in one way or another!"

"Right. I'll be along in twenty minutes," said the Superintendent, briskly. "With a few men. Meet me there, Frederick. Good heavens – this all sounds *quite* impossible!"

Fatty put down the telephone and turned to Ern, who was listening nearby. "Ring up the others for me, Ern," he said. "Tell them to meet us at Fairlin Hall quickly – even if they're in the middle of breakfast. This is going to be exciting. I'm going to get some biscuits for poor old Buster – he'll be starving!"

In fifteen minutes' time Larry, Daisy, Pip, Bets and Ern were all in the drive of Fairlin Hall, in a state of the greatest excitement. Fatty was at the gate waiting for the Superintendent and his men. Ah – here they come in two black police cars. The Superintendent jumped out and said a few words to the man with him. Then he strode toward Fatty.

"Now let's get down to business," he said, clapping Fatty on the back. "Lead on!"

"We'd better rescue poor Mr. Goon first," said Fatty. "And Buster too. I'm afraid Mr. Goon will be in a fearful temper, sir."

"That won't matter," said the Superintendent hard-heartedly, "Hallo, Bets! You here! And all the others too! Well, I'm blessed!"

They all went to the kitchen door and Fatty pushed it open. A loud barking was coming from the locked cupboard. Fatty went over and unlocked it. Out leapt Buster, mad with joy at seeing Fatty again, and being free once more.

"Steady, Buster, steady," said Fatty. There came a noise from the cupboard and Mr. Goon walked out, looking as if he was about to burst with rage! He advanced on Fatty.

"*You're* at the bottom of this!" he roared. "Toad of a boy! And you, Ern, what do you mean by getting me here in the middle of the night, and ... oh ... er ... good morning, Superintendent. Didn't see you, I'm afraid. I've got a complaint to lay against this Frederick Trotteville. Always interfering with the law, he is, sir. After I'd settled a case, he goes on with it, poking his nose in, and ..."

"That's enough, Goon, for the moment," said the Superintendent. "Where are these other men, did you say, Frederick?"

Goon looked astounded. Other men? What did the Superintendent mean? He followed Fatty and the others out into the yard. A voice came from the coal-cellar.

"Let us out! One of us has a broken ankle. We give up!"

Goon stared in surprise at the dustbin full of big stones, as one of the policemen heaved it off the grating. He stared even more when the grating was taken off too, and a constable shouted down into the cellar.

"Come on up – you're wanted for questioning. We know you're the fellows in that Diamond Case years ago."

The men had to be dragged up, because the ladder had broken in half. Goon was overcome with astonishment. What *was* all this?

"We can explain everything," said one of the men.

"You've got nothing on us. We only came back here to visit the old place – to see old Mrs. Hasterley."

"People don't live in empty houses," said the Superintendent curtly. "Frederick – we'll all go somewhere and talk over this, I think."

"There's nothing to talk about," interrupted Goon. "It's just a case I cleared up myself. These fellows sent notes to me, telling me about a caretaker here – man run in for being a traitor – and . . ."

"Sir – could we go into Fairlin Hall for a few minutes?" said Fatty. "There's still a little matter to be cleared up there, if you don't mind. We could go into the kitchen."

"Very well," said the Superintendent, and he and Goon, and all the children filed in. The Superintendent sat down in the old arm-chair.

"You know all about that long ago diamond affair, sir," began Fatty. "Well, as soon as those two fellows you caught just now got together, when one of them came out of prison, they decided to come back here and find the diamond haul, which Wilfrid Hasterley had hidden safely away. They found caretakers in the kitchen quarters, so they couldn't search. They then discovered that Mr. Smith, the caretaker, had a shady past – had sold some secret papers to a foreign government . . ."

"And I turned them out of here!" said Goon. "Quite right, too. Couldn't have a fellow . . ."

"Quiet, Goon," said the Superintendent. "Go on, Frederick."

"Well, as Mr. Goon said, he turned them out – and so left the place clear for the two thieves to search," said Fatty, "which is exactly what they wanted! Well, *we* were on the trail, as well – we knew about the messages to Goon, you see – and we guessed the two fellows were after the hidden diamonds. So we came to search too!"

"Gah!" said Goon, in disgust.

"Well, we didn't find them. But last night I came back here again, and the men were here too – and to cut a long story short, sir, Ern here imprisoned the two men in the coal-cellar, got me out of a cupboard where I'd been locked, and ..."

"But how did *Goon* get locked in?" said the Superintendent, looking suspiciously at Ern.

"Oooh, *I* didn't lock my uncle in," said Ern, hastily. "I wouldn't do such a thing. The *men* locked him in, sir."

"And did those fellows give you any hint as to where the diamonds were?" asked the Superintendent, looking at Fatty expectantly.

"No, sir," said Fatty. Everyone groaned – what a pity! No diamonds after all!

"Well – that's rather an anti-climax," said the Superintendent, looking disappointed. "*Sure* you don't know where they are, Frederick?"

"Well – yes, sir, I think I *do* know where they are – though I haven't *seen* them!" said Fatty.

WHAT a sensation that made! Everyone gaped at Fatty, and the Superintendent stood up at once.

"You *know* where they're hidden!" he said. "You actually *know*?"

"Well – I can make a jolly good guess," said Fatty. "If I were a plumber I could find out at once."

"A *plumber*? What do you mean?" said the Superintendent. "Come on, Frederick – no more mystery, please!"

"Well, sir – come into the bathroom," said Fatty, and everyone squeezed into the tiny bathroom, even Goon. Fatty tapped the cold-water pipe, that still sent out a tiny drip at the loose joint.

"I think the diamonds are all jammed into this pipe, sir," he said. "It was Mrs. Smith who first mentioned the pipe to me – she said the flow of water was very poor indeed. Then when I examined it, I saw that the joint was loose – it's been badly done, sir, if you look – not a professional job at all. And I just put two and two together, sir, and thought. 'Well, this is about the only place where nobody's looked! They must be here!'"

139

"Can't be!" said the Superintendent, staring at the pipe. "What an idea! But what a hiding-place! What do *you* think, Goon?"

"Diamonds in a water-pipe?" said Goon, scornfully, delighted at being asked his advice. "Never heard of such a thing in my life. You have that pipe cut, sir – we'll flood the bathroom, but that's about all we'll do!"

The Superintendent went to the door and called out to one of his men. "Get that hack-saw of yours, Sergeant!"

"Right, sir!" And in half a minute in came the Sergeant with an efficient-looking little saw.

"I want that pipe cut," said the Superintendent, nodding his head at the little water-pipe. "The water's turned off, so there's only what's in the pipes. Cut below that loose joint, where the water's dripping a little."

Everyone watched while the Sergeant did a little sawing – then water spurted out – and with it came two small sparkling things that fell to the ground, and lay there, glittering. Fatty pounced on them at once, and dropped them into the Superintendent's hand.

"Whew! Yes – they're diamonds all right," he said. "The pipe must be crammed with them! No wonder the water wouldn't flow through properly. Cut another place, Sergeant."

The man obeyed – and there was no doubt of it, the pipe was full of diamonds – some big, some small, none of them any the worse for having lain in water for so many years.

"Sergeant – take a couple of men and empty the pipe," ordered the Superintendent, looking extremely pleased. "Frederick – you deserve a medal for this! Good work, my boy – as good as any you've ever done. Don't you think so, Goon?"

Goon didn't think so. Goon was busy blowing his nose loudly. Goon didn't want to answer *any* questions about Fatty at all. He was tired to death of Fatty and Ern, and all he wanted to do was to go home and have a Nice Hot Cup of Tea.

"I'll have to come and take a report about all this from you, Frederick, some time or other," said the Superintendent, his hand on Fatty's shoulder. "But now I must go and question those two men. My warm congratulations – and if I were you, I'd go and put something on that frightful bruise. One of the men did that, I uppose?"

"Yes. But I don't mind!" said Fatty. "I gave as good as I got. Gosh – it *was* a night and a half, sir – and Ern here did as much as I did. More!"

"My congratulations to you too, Ern," said the Superintendent. "I shouldn't be surprised if you didn't have a little Something coming to you as a reward for your good work."

Ern blushed all over his face in surprise and delight. How he longed to be like Fatty, and let his "tongue go loose". What a "pome" he would recite to the Superintendent! But all he could say was, "I'm going to be a policeman some day, sir – and I'll be a Sergeant in no time at all – you see if I don't!"

"Gah!" said Goon, before he could stop himself, and marched off angrily. That Ern! And to think he'd given him five shillings for helping him. What a waste!

"Let's all go back and have breakfast at my house," said Fatty. "I'm starving. Mother will have a fit when she sees my bruise! Gosh, I do hope it doesn't go down before I'm back at school – I'll be the envy of everyone when I tell them how I got it. Well, Ern – how did you enjoy *this* Mystery?"

"Loveaduck!" said Ern, beaming. "It was Smashing, Fatty. Thanks a lot for letting me in on it. Never enjoyed myself so much in my life. And don't forget – I've still got that five shillings left that my uncle gave me. I'll stand you all ice-creams this morning, and that goes for Buster too!"

"Good old Ern," said Fatty, and clapped him on the shoulder. And the others all said the same, making the boy blush as red as a beetroot. "Good Old Ern."

141

Have you read all the adventures in the "Mystery" series by Enid Blyton?

The Rockingdown Mystery

Roger, Diana, Snubby and Barney hear strange noises in the cellar while staying at Rockingdown Hall. Barney goes to investigate and makes a startling discovery . . .

The Rilloby Fair Mystery

Valuable papers have disappeared – the Green Hands Gang has struck again! Which of Barney's workmates at the circus is responsible? The four friends turn detectives – and have to tackle a dangerous criminal.

The Ring O'Bells Mystery

Eerie things happen at deserted Ring O'Bells Hall – bells start to ring, strange noises are heard in a secret passage, and there are some very unfriendly strangers about. Something very mysterious is going on and the friends mean to find out what . . .

The Rubadub Mystery

Who is the enemy agent at the top-secret submarine harbour? Roger, Diana, Snubby and Barney are determined to find out – and find themselves involved in a most exciting mystery.

The Rat-A-Tat Mystery

When the big knocker on the ancient door of Rat-A-Tat House bangs by itself in the middle of the night, it heralds a series of very peculiar happenings – and provides another action-packed adventure for Roger, Diana, Snubby and Barney.

The Ragamuffin Mystery

"This is going to be the most exciting holiday we've ever had," said Roger – and little does he know how true his words will prove when he and his three friends go to Merlin's Cove and discover the hideout of a gang of thieves.

Armada

Have you read all the "Secrets" stories by Enid Blyton?

THE SECRET ISLAND

Peggy, Mike and Nora are having a miserable time with
unkind Aunt Harriet and Uncle Henry – until they make
friends with wild Jack and discover the secret island.

THE SECRET OF SPIGGY HOLES

On a holiday by the sea, Mike, Jack, Peggy and Nora
discover a secret passage – and a royal prisoner in a sinister
cliff-top house. The children plan to free the young prince
– and take him to the secret island.

THE SECRET MOUNTAIN

Jack, Peggy, Nora and Mike team up with Prince Paul of
Baronia to search for their parents, who have been
kidnapped and taken to the secret mountain. Their daring
rescue mission seems doomed to failure – especially when
the children are captured and one of them is to be sacrificed
to the sun-god.

THE SECRET OF KILLIMOOIN

When Prince Paul invited Nora, Mike, Peggy and Jack to
spend the summer holidays with him in Baronia, they were
thrilled. By amazing luck, they find the hidden entrance to
the Secret Forest – but can they find their way out?

THE SECRET OF MOON CASTLE

Moon Castle is said to have had a violent, mysterious past
so Jack, Peggy, Mike and Nora are wildly excited when
Prince Paul's family rent it for the holidays. When weird
things begin to happen, the children are determined to
know the strange secrets the castle hides . . .

Armada

THE MYSTERY THAT NEVER WAS

by

Enid Blyton

Don't miss this exciting adventure story by the world's best-ever storyteller!

Nicky decides to invent a mystery for his Uncle Bob — a private investigator — to solve. But there's a nasty shock in store for Nicky. When spooky lights signal in the night from the old mansion on Skylark Hill, he realises that his mystery is coming horrifyingly true.

Armada